HERO

HERO

JEREMY NICHOLAS

Grey Wolfe Publishing, LLC
PO Box 1088
Birmingham, Michigan 48009
www.GreyWolfePublishing.com

© 2013 Jeremy Nicholas
Published by Grey Wolfe Publishing, LLC
www.GreyWolfePublishing.com
All Rights Reserved

First Edition ISBN: 978-1-62828-019-7
Second Edition ISBN: 978-1-62828-160-6
Library of Congress Control Number: 2013954820

DEDICATION

Philip Ray Nicholas

To the man that taught me:

1. How to fish, "six twists and loop it through."
2. How to hunt, "Shoot it! Shoot it! Stop! You're shootin' at the house!"
3. How to handle getting a shot at the doctor's office, "Hurting is Helping."
4. How to get her back, "She's right, Son."

To the man that showed me everything from how to be a good father to how to lose your father with grace and dignity.

To the man that has forgiven me when nobody else would have and stood in my corner when it was an awfully lonely place to be.

To the man that taught me what a real man was; that they could be tough and still treat people fair, that it is my job to support my family and not so much their job to support me.

To the greatest man in the world, hands down. All you other fellas take a back seat. My dad is my Hero because he earned it.

ACKNOWLEDGEMENTS

I have been blessed beyond words, to the point that the names of these people cannot all be printed because they simply would not fit.

Jessiy (Peach) Nicholas: There is only one of you and then they broke the mold. I cannot thank you enough for the support you give and the thankless jobs you endure by being my wife and the mother to our children. You are the true measure of a woman and anyone that is not aspiring to be more like you, has missed the point of being amazing because you define it and embody a power that few understand, man or woman. I love you, Peach.

Brenda (Mom) Nicholas: Though we see eye to eye about poppy seed chicken, chocolate chip pecan pie and little else, I love you and I would never be the man I am today without the beautiful love you gave me all of my life. Thank you for protecting me even when I didn't want you to. Thank you for teaching me standards and thank you most of all for setting a standard in my own mind about how much I am worth and how I should expect others to treat me, especially women.

Lisa Kee: Never did a teacher maintain a classroom with your grace. She was a soft spoken woman, years ahead of the profession to which she gave her entire life, as far as I am concerned. She cursed me with the need to chase windmills like Don Quixote, to love as blindly as did he and to write like my life depended on it.

John Staniloiu, Kayleen Starbright Staniloiu, Jane Suarez, Erin, Joshua, Shawn, Chris, Wildflower, Ashley, Charles, Brenda, Apple Annie, Larry, Laurel, Josh, Linda, Udo, Sage, Deb N, Debbie, and a few faces to which I cannot put a name,

The time I spent with you at Phoenix Ranch changed my life forever. You may have never known that it did. But your way of life was completely foreign to me when I came to the place that we have in common. Not all those times were easy. However, here are a few I will take to my grave happily:

-   Fishing, Caving, Sweats, Laughter, Hitchhiking, family dinners, car-hood sled rides, horseback riding, singing, hearts (the game), petrified owl heads, Vision Quests, Homemade Wine, Gardening, "Construction" Projects, Naps, Hugs.

When I left, part of me died. I stayed very angry about that for years and I miss you all today. A few of you have gone on and I will never see you again. It breaks my heart. But, it was good to spend pretend time with each of you as I wrote this novel.

The Traditional Lakota and Their Sacred Lodge

I feel it very necessary to mention that while I do loosely use this traditional sacred ceremony throughout this story, I want the Lakota people to understand that I mean no offense whatsoever. White people have been doing lodges for decades and while I understand that some of the Lakota people feel offended by that, please let it be an honor that some white people are finding your way intriguing and looking for hope on the "Red Road" rather than in the politically charged churches that motivated a government years ago, to segregate you and destroy your scared way of life by making many of the traditions you held illegal.

I hope that I portray the lodge in this account as something you can be proud of, a wisdom that has crossed the boarders that my ancestors drew out, long before me. Let me be clear that I cannot apologize for portraying your ancient practice in a modern setting. So, I will not. To apologize would be like apologizing for spreading peace and transcendence. Nor am I apologizing for what people I never met did to your people. What I will apologize for is that we still do it to you today.

In August, I visited Wounded Knee. I had read about it and in doing so, had no preconceptions about it being something grand like the Crazy Horse monument, less than one hundred miles away. What I was unprepared for and what threw me to the Earth like a mighty blow from a hard right hand, was that I was standing on the graves of the men women and children that were slaughtered not very long ago. Whether it be a mistake made by a few terrified young boys under the direction of their leader or an intentional massacre bred of hate and discontent, it was, no doubt a massacre and fear played and enormous part.

During this story, I really try to tackle fear and why it breeds the behavior that it does. I was so moved by Wounded Knee and by my own experiences in at least a rendition of your sacred ceremony that I had to include it in this account. Please bear with me in my ignorance as to the weight that ceremony holds for you and I beg your permission to let me use it as an example of calling upon the Earth and its powerful elements to heal this torn nation that has only used it for its resources and never, never stopped to consider that she may be fed up with us.

PROLOGUE

Hero fell hard on the dry grass like a heavy feed sack. The thud of his fall, he felt deep in his bones. The ache burned and throbbed and every pore screamed for relief. He used his waning twisted muscles to slowly turn his head around. He wondered how far he would have to pull himself to get the relief that only the cool shade could offer under a tree. It was still at least thirty feet. It would be thirty feet of painful torture to get any respite from the grueling sun. It was thirty feet too many. Hero couldn't muster the strength to move another inch. He had managed to slow the blood earlier when he tried to rest. He had tried clotting it with his once white t-shirt. But, in his panicky race to get somewhere, anywhere, he was pumping blood like a coughing spicket from his broken sternum. His shirt was fruitless as good clotting material. It was full of fresh warm blood, enough to be rung out.

Somehow, being shot always seemed an honorable death. The movies he had seen displayed it proudly, the good guy laying in the street bleeding out his heart and bleeding his last goodbyes from a stiff lip to the beautiful lady holding his head as she cried for him. This felt anything but honorable. There were no beautiful women to hold his head. The only things he could utter were bloody gurgling moans and salty, lonely tears. Desperate fear filled every cell of his being. *What a stupid thing to say!* He thought. *Honorable death! What death is honorable?*

He lay there, panting every breath. He was exuding precious moisture and energy from his body and couldn't control it. He thought, *This is it. This is the sum of my life.* He thought of all the people he had met. He wondered if they might be thinking of him in this instance. *Did I leave them with a happy thought of me or are they angry by anything I may have done? Are they thinking, 'That crazy boy! What an idiot!' Or have I lived up to my name? Am I a Hero?*

The bright sun had shrouded itself with a dark cloak and now showed itself as a shrinking point of light in his eyes only. His breaths grew shallow. His body still heaved in the futile attempt to breathe precious air. His back arched and his fingers clenched upon themselves in the throes of death. Smaller and smaller, the point of light slipped away and his breathing halted abruptly. No more sight. No more sensations of touch save a faint tingle in his feet. His body could not move. His muscles were rigid and useless. For the first time in his life, he recognized and felt his own brainwaves coursing in a frantic rush to save his life. They were electricity channeling through his head. They moved like pin balls at the speed of lightning. But, they could find no hole in which to sink and rest and affect the nervous system. He had never been more aware than in this moment of his functioning mind. It is strange that only in dis-function do we ever really realize how we functioned before. But, it was to no avail. A final dry exhale was his only goodbye. It was his last words of love. That lonely breath outward toward the ether from whence he came, was Hero's final call to the life that he left behind. Hero passed on.

The grass was wet now and the air was cool. It was completely black and not a sound was heard. There were no trumpets. There were no gates. No reward awaited him. He was not even him anymore. He did not exist. Hero was gone and only the broken body of a once resilient man lay crumpled in the dew soaking it up.

Jack looked down at the man and thought, *It's over now.* The Shadow was pleased. It was enthralled with hope for a new beginning. But Jack was empty. He was empty and alone, nothing but a shell, a host feeding the Shadow that controlled his every move.

CHAPTER ONE

Jack leapt into the air and flung a strong grasp onto the passing boxcar's ledge. His heavy pack weighed him down. Once he knew for sure that he was securely attached to the swift moving train, he hurled the pack over his shoulder, around his body and finally into the dark, empty car. This always appeared to be such a feat when he told his mother how he traveled. But in reality, it was much less graceful. Jack didn't jump onto trains the way they did in the movies. Nor did he do it with any real grace. No one did. In fact, most boarded the moving beasts when they were stopped. Only a few crazy wanderers like Jack, jumped haphazardly upon the moving machinery like their life depended on the ride. Jack had lost his things on occasion. Usually, it was blamed on thievery. Often a boxcar only appeared to be empty and Jack would have to watch over his things closely, guarding them from fellow riders. Not everyone on the rail is friendly. In fact, few are. Occasionally, things were lost as Jack would fling his bag inside the car and, in concert fall off the rattling, smoking beast. Jack had even seen a few men lose grip and fall, only to be sliced up by the hard shining rails and the big turning wheels. The railroad men hated them for this, not inherently, of course. They were taught to hate them by the big men that signed their paychecks. They saw it as a liability. They were afraid that some desperate family member from far away would get it in their head to sue the railroad over the foolish decision of a distant family member to ride the rail instead of traveling in a car like the rest of the human race, which resulted in their gruesome death. Rarely does the wanderer wish to sue the rail. They know going in, the train can be dangerous and that is half of the excitement. They love the train. It is their greatest ally. But sometimes even your greatest ally may strike back at you and end it all. This is a dichotomy that any good hobo lives with, happily. This time was success and Jack swung himself as best he could into the big empty steel box. It was a cold night. He was alone. More often than not, when traveling like this, it is good to be alone. Not to say that everyone you meet on the tracks is dangerous. But some are and some are just plain annoying. All kinds of people travel this way, from vagrants and vagabonds to victors and vicarious wannabes.

Jack found a corner with the least amount of wind rushing through, unfurled his sleeping mat and stretched it out. He was exhausted. There was very little light pouring in from the late afternoon. What was left of the big bright sun was being hidden by an overcast blanket that Jack had been living under for weeks. Only moments ago, Jack had left his beloved Memphis. He had been here for several months, living on the streets, hustling any kind money he could by day labor and playing a little guitar outside the Daisy, one of Beale Street's oldest stages. But it was time to move on because the town he held so dear changed with the cold. The local people were tough, determined and kept the air as alive as they could. But the tourists had moved on to warmer weather. They would be back in April. Until then, Jack had a place to go and the way was by train. He sat in the boxcar and contemplated his time in town and thought of what locals would do in his absence. He was certain things would go just fine without him.

It was November. Memphis had recently seen an unusually warm string of falls. But this was more true to form. It was cold and bleak. Brisk mornings gave way to slightly warmer afternoons. But, in the late evening, the cold settled back down on the streets that never got the opportunity to warm enough for the bare foot children. In years before, the children were called in from playing out on the dirty street to eat turkey, dressing, and collard greens. This year, they would hover around the warm oven and wait for the Thanksgiving meal to be done. "Black Jesus", framed in homage, hangs on the wall and looks over the mothers and their babies and only the men dare tough the outside cold in order to smoke a cigar and have a sip of whiskey. They would speak in their southern drawls to one another and yell back into the house, complimenting the wonderful smells of turkey that filled the air. Football is in full swing and the radio would announce each play with excitement.

Tonight, the blues men play a little sadder in the bars and almost never on the streets. The tourists aren't as impressed and are more likely to complain to somebody about the fact that they were hoping for the "Real Memphis". But, the food wasn't as good as last time or the blues man was drunk when he performed. Likewise, the waitress is more likely to cry and the blues man is more likely to order his drummer to fling a drumstick at the out-of-towner's head.

Jack had spent the night before with a group of travelers that intended on catching the New Orleans train that was southbound. They were heading for warmer weather, for easier panhandling and hustling, where the tourists were still drunk and happy. Jack wanted to go with them something awful. But, he had a commitment to fulfill and his heart was longing for the Ozark Hills, their burnt autumn colors and cold streams with places still seldom touched by man's destructive ingenuity. He had promised Eli that he would be there for the last cut of dwindling hay and had already missed that appointment. However, he knew his friend well and was doubtful that all the winter preparations had been made. He was certain Eli would be logging partly for cash and mostly for firewood. Jack knew he could make up for his absence by being helpful in this way. He wanted to fish, as well. Jack could easily lose an entire day sitting by the flowing water, casting his line, letting it drift and pulling it in. Every half an hour to an hour there was a tug, a short battle and the possibility of success. Sometimes he threw them back. He occasionally stoked a small fire and fried the filets in hot grease for lunch. Many days, he spent with his line in the water and not fishing at all. Instead, he would only gaze to the bluffs, with their haunting caves where he had slept peacefully, amazed at how their mouths opened to the river as if they would drink it up.

His friend's ranch teemed with all sorts of beautiful life. There were white tail deer, bald eagles, wild horses and beauty in small forms like the spring-time morel mushrooms and slopes covered in ginseng. The people there were a bit different from him. They were careful to coexist with the world around them instead of conquering it. Jack much preferred conquering at his young age. But, he loved the people there and could easily see himself as one of them at an older age, a little less full of what his friends referred to as "piss and vinegar".

****

The wheels clinked along down the track as Jack made his way out of Memphis. There was no song but the whining rails. He felt a jolt from the head end of the train and he knew they were crossing the Mississippi. Slowly, Jack left his snug sleeping bag and crawled to the door of this rattle-trap temporary home. He stuck his head out cautiously and faced the brisk oncoming breeze. He could see the lights of a barge. It was definitely moving. But it appeared to be sitting still in the water. Jack wondered to himself why barges must move so slowly. He thought it to be a conspiracy against economic development. *Surely they could make those things really go. Ya' know, get it on down the river. But, No! They gotta' drag ass and make sure every man's got his chance to make a dollar.* He didn't mind a man making a dollar. Jack just thought there was an awful lot of waste going on so that big men could make big dollars. Jack wanted no part of that "circle of doom" as he phrased it. So, his lot was to ride the rails and work only for what he needed to live.

The Mississippi was wide and full from an unusually rainy fall. It rushed around the large bends, as smooth as glass on top. Even so, Jack knew there was a terrible hell of turbulence down below. He had heard before that the undertow of the Mississippi would pull a man to the bottom in a second flat and pin him there until she decided to spew his lifeless body out upon her sandy bank. It was as if she punished him for being arrogant enough to cross her. Not only would she kill him; but the mighty river even went to the trouble of disposing of the body she had ruthlessly drowned. Jack was enthralled with her mystery and he wanted desperately to hear her roaring below. But, there was no sound except the rail's lonesome scream and the clinking wheels pounding away at the track. At that point, he seriously thought about jumping off right after the bridge and walking up or down river. He thought it a shame to ride over the river all these times and never get the chance to spend any time listening to her. Maybe he would just get as far from the city as he could, sit down and build a little fire and try to catch some sleep. *Tomorrow, maybe I could build a raft and fish like Tom or Huck or whichever it was. No!* Jack thought; *I'll build a raft and teach them damn barges how to haul cargo across the river!* He knew he would do neither. Jack was going to Missouri. It was time to make good on his word and step away from the tracks for a little while.

The car clunked hard on the rail as he left the bridge and the Mississippi behind. A new cold set in that had a twinge of fear embedded inside it. The fear dug deep into Jacks chest and he threw himself back into the dark car, finding his sleeping bag. He curled up in it and pretended to be back over the familiar Mississippi. He closed his eyes and pretended that the bridge hadn't ended. In fact, it went on for as long as he would sleep. He refused the existence of the presence of darkness that rested in a corner of the boxcar. That black spot could never be real and certainly wasn't a friend of his. This lonesome traveler appeared to have a companion, an unwanted companion, but, a companion nonetheless. Sleep it away, Jack. Just close your eyes and sleep it away. When he woke, there would be no cold dark boxcar hurling itself into the black Arkansas night. The black spot in the car would be revealed as some graffiti left over from younger rail riders and thugs. The sun would be out and would have warmed the cold and lonely car. He would be able to stick his head out again into the inviting, crisp fall air and watch the Hardy hills pass by. He could wink at the girls sunbathing at Big Spring as his car sailed by and on to My Hope. *Wait it is November! There will be no sunbathing girls!* But, he kept these thoughts in his mind and soon, he calmed down enough to let his mind rest. Sleep settled finally. He couldn't remember his last thoughts as he fell deeper into sweet unconsciousness. He awoke several times with the bumps and bangs throughout the night, falling right back to sleep as he followed his dreams to the west.

****

Jack awoke to the familiar song of the rail which all good hobos know as a high pitched whine, haunting like a love that never lets a man go. She follows him into his dreams and chases him awake again only to conquer his daydreams as well. He pilfers papers at work only to appear to be doing anything at all while he speaks to her under the desk as if she is his own. But, he can never own her. She owns him. Many men have shed good jobs and shattered their loving families to ride the wicked rail and Jack figures it must be that damn whine. She whines and she whines until you come back to rest in her cars again, to drink cold coffee and lukewarm canned soup in her train yard, to sleep on a hard car's board floor, to be subject to the winter chill and suffer the sweltering summer heat in a box car. She offers more pain and despair, more fear and lonesomeness than any woman. But, men like Jack cannot divorce her because she is in their veins. They run to her in the night.

The rail also offers the view before him now and this is when she is sweet, so sweet. The yellow sun crests the big leaf sycamores that hang white in their tops over the Big Spring River. He sees an early morning fisherman alone and waist deep in the blue spring water. His stringer is floating a few feet downstream, loaded with wiggling brown trout. The fisherman exhales a puff of his cigarette. The smoke portrays him as something iconic and legendary. Man, his net, and poles out in the cold fall morning harnessing the world around him, no matter how wild. He moves like Jack's father in the water, fluid and strong. He is careful not to let his fly lay on the water long enough to sink. He whips the fly lure back and forth to mimic the twitching insect and in many ways becomes the fly bouncing around the water. He is in his element. He feels, for a moment, he can dance on the water just as his fly can. The water breaks quickly and the fly is consumed from the blue abyss. Lead, lead, lead, lead... And... Snap! The fisherman pulls up and back hard; the fly rod bends dramatically, obeying the strain of a big trout that just bit. A big grin comes across the fisherman's face. Jack loses control and yells, "Whoooohooo!" The fisherman looks up and Jack remembers that screaming from the train isn't all too wise and hurries back into the belly of the car. A few seconds pass and he crawls back out like a commando in the jungle, eyes peeled for anyone who may have seen him. The coast appears clear.

Jack turns his attention upstream and up track. Just as he thought! He knew the water was awfully blue! He has almost arrived at The Big Spring. The train will stop just a few miles north, as there is a small no name stop there. But, Jack likes to jump early at the spring to save getting caught by the brutes on the engineer's big expensive train. He's taken a beating twice before and now he tries to always jump a little early.

Jack hurries back into the old friendly boxcar and rolls up his mat. He ties it to the bottom of his pack and quickly stuffs his thin wool army blanket down into the old pack. His pack was beautiful to him. It was a key to freedom, green like the grass he walked on, tattered and patched like his soul, and dirty like his clothes. Jack's father taught him to always be certain his pack was full of the necessities and as little frills as possible. Jack's father wasn't a traveling man. But, he was an outdoorsman and his back-pack skill had served Jack well over the last few years.

Standing upright now, he holds the pack out in front of him and waits for a tree line to block any onlooker's view. He looks back in\to the train. The black spot is still there. It wasn't graffiti after all. But, Jack cannot concern himself with this. He is too ready to jump and get on with his adventure to the ranch. A good, solid tree line rushes upon him quickly with the speed of the moving train, just an amber and red blur. Jack lunges forward, pushing hard off the boxcar floor and into the open morning air while simultaneously dropping the pack below him. This is freedom for a moment. There is no train. There is no track, no whine. There is only air and he is flying in it. Reality can settle itself in momentarily. But for now, Jack is not Jack. He is flying Super Jack. When his body crashes to the gravel below, Jack rolls and skids alongside his pack until they both come crashing to a halt, stopping shortly before the roots of the trees that hid his presence a moment earlier.

Lying still for a moment to make sure no one saw him jump; Jack listens as the sounds of the Missouri-Arkansas border come to life. First, the birds singing and then the water rushing, followed by the faint sounds of the people playing at Big Spring begin to fill his ears. They are familiar and welcome. They are warm and inviting him to play along. But Jack knows to stay away from the town-folk initially, at least until he bathes and can stash his pack somewhere so as to not look homeless. He walks about two hundred yards through the brush lifting heavy foot after foot. The withering vines grab at him as if to hold him in place, making Jack a permanent monument to the forest. If the vines had their way, he would be frozen forever in one of the many small batches of trees along the track. His pots clang together in his pack and the lack of a good breakfast begins to obsess his thoughts.

As he approaches the final opening of trees, he doubles back and finds a clearing to start a small fire and heat his beans. Normally, he would eat them cold. But the ranch is only a day or so away by foot and if he is lucky, he could be bedding down there tonight, if he can hitch a ride. Jack figures, *eating now certainly won't hurt my chances of going hungry any time soon and taking the time to make a hot meal is equally as un-detrimental to my timeframe. Anyway, if something did go wrong, I am by a river and a spring.* Jack remembered clearly what his father taught him. "A spring is good to drink from, for you and the animal you want to eat."

The small fire crackles and the gooey can of chili beans sitting on top of it bubbles and steams. Jack likes to cook and eat out of the can because it saves doing many dishes. He grabs the spoon out of his pack pocket and dives in with ferocious hunger. The stale crackers are left alone just in case he is in need of an emergency snack. The chili beans are his total focus until they are gone. *Waste nothing*, he thinks to himself. *As a traveler, one must think in terms of calories instead of full or not full.* Jack had difficulty thinking in terms of calories, though. He had no fancy machine to tell him what he needed to eat, how much, and when to conserve. So, he went by his common sense. *Learn to sleep hungry. Eat ferociously before you toil hard and do not eat just for something to do. Every calorie in my body must be guaranteed to get me where I need to be, safely. To eat a whole pack of crackers just because one is bored and has nothing going on, would be an idiotic waste and to not eat a can of beans before possibly having to walk thirty miles would be equally as idiotic.*

Water is equally an absolute commodity. Without it, the human body will perish quicker than with the absence of any other element, aside from oxygen. Every clean water source warrants a fill up or top off of the vital fluid. Jack knows this and with half a canteen of water, peers through the Sycamores at the cold clear water of Big Spring. There are children playing around it. Normally, he would wait until they left to avoid any contact with the law. But, he has only a little to go and then he is home free at the beloved ranch that he misses so dearly.

Jack climbs from the tangled brush. It continues to pull at his feet. But he is successful at breaking free and snaps the dying fall vines with a quick forceful step. In front of him, the water pumps from the earth, thousands of gallons per minute being forced out of the bedrock, cold and blue as the sky. Jack approaches the gigantic spring and thrusts his canteen deep into it until it fills up. On his hands and knees, he reaches into the water and splashes his face and neck. As Jack stands, the cool fall air blows against his skin and he feels invigorated and alive.

The children all mind their own except for one boy who is staring at him like he is some weird alien man. That child's mother snatches him up quickly and jerks him away. Jack thought to himself, *you're next little man*. Jack knows that being snatched away from what intrigues a child, only drives the child to chase it with intent and purpose when he becomes a man. Jack's mother did the same thing. She loved him dearly. She shrouded him from anything that could hurt him. That strained their relationship as Jack was a teen. In fact, it strained his mother's and his father's relationship with one another.

When Jack's mother finally let go, she bestowed upon him the little Bible that he carries in his pack to this day. Jack doesn't truly believe any of the stories that it tells. However, it has brought comfort at some darker times in his life. It has cured boredom when there was nothing else to read. Furthermore, he'd used all the blank pages as rolling papers when he ran out once or twice. He would never tell his mother that, though. He would just say, "Yes ma'am, I've been keeping up with it."

"Boy, keeping up with it aint doing you no good."

"I read on it every once in a while, Momma."

"Well, ya better be reading an awful lot of it, boy. I just don't understand how you live this way."

So, the story goes. Jack is woefully accustomed to it and knows his momma will never change. He had tried a few times to talk with her about the world as he sees it and how that book is just exactly that, a book, like any other. To Jack, it is a book full of great parables and stories. But it is full of contradictions, just the same, and he feared that there must've been some mistake and wondered, *does that mistake make the whole thing screwed up?* He grew so tired of the constant investigation it took to understand things such as salvation; he figured he must be saved. Jack was a good guy. He didn't rob, steal, kill and tried hard to treat his neighbors like he wanted to be treated. He didn't attend any services because he saw the same folks running in and out of the Memphis brothels and bars that he had frequented as well. But, come Sunday, there they were in the pew, with the pretend smiles and their broken family in tow. Jack wanted nothing of this and knew something had to be wrong with the picture.

Jack turns to the north and looks ahead. Ahead is his destination. Picking up the heavy pack, He begins to walk up from the spring toward the road. The dying grass crunches under his feet and he trudges upward until his old leather boots reach the pavement. The pavement is warm as it should be from the sun. The grass and ground never really get warm in the winter. But the pavement seems to warm up no matter what time of year it is as long as the sun is there to warm it. Jack has slept on it before for that reason. It was the warmest place he could find.

His heavy boots tramp hard against the warm asphalt intent on reaching the place he has dreamed of for a long summer in the south. The northbound traffic wizzes by him, not noticing his thumb is in the air. If he doesn't catch a ride soon, he'll be sleeping along-side the road. That would be fine had he not had his hopes alive with sleeping in a comfy bed tonight. "I should've known it wouldn't be this easy." Jack waked some five miles straight uphill toward the plains west of Thomasville and still remained almost twenty miles from his best chance for a ride if no one was going to pick him up along-side the highway.

He sat down and the depression shrouded down upon him. *I'm gonna be doing this for days!* He thought. *What the hell is anybody gonna pick up a hobo for, sitting here, dirty and smelling like rotten whiskey and body odor!*

While Jack sat there, miserable on the pavement, he looked south down the hill that he just climbed and turned back north immediately. He felt defeated and exhausted when he heard the sound of brakes squeaking behind him. Jack turned back to the south and a little red Honda was stopping on the shoulder of the highway. He peered through the dirty windshield and could only see the silhouette of a woman. The car came to a complete stop and the woman appeared to simply sit there. Jack thought she must have broken down. *What an unfortunate girl to break down here, having only to witness me in my misery on the side of the road.* Jack sunk his head between his bent knees and waited for her to make her phone call from inside her car for help. Women rarely picked Jack up when he thumbed it. If they did, it was a group of them. So, he never even considered this to be an offer for a ride to anywhere. But to his surprise, the door flung open and out stepped a dark haired young girl about his age. She was beautiful. Her hair blew back in the November wind and Jack sat there speechless. He though that she must be lost and may ask directions only to leave him on the warm pavement and make her way as politely as possible to the next town.

But she did none of that. "Are you getting in or just going to sit there like a whipped dog?" she said.

Jack stammered over his words and ended up making something audible and understandable, come from his open jaw. "I do, do not. I will. . . Thank you." He said. She just laughed at him and motioned him to the little red car. Jack gathered his scattered things and made his way to the passenger door. She opened it for him from the inside and popped the trunk. Jack asked if he could please, at least keep his things in the back seat instead of the trunk, and she asked, "Why?"

Jack explained to the girl, "look I'm not here to hurt you and you don't have to give me a ride anyways. I've had my pack leave in a trunk or two and I'd rather be able to grab it quick if you throw me out. You're welcome to go through it and make sure it's all okay." He didn't really want her going through his things. But he wouldn't dare deny her the opportunity if she so chose. He knew it would make her feel more comfortable.

However, the girl chose not to look through his things. She just looked at him bewildered and said, "You poor thing. It is mighty pathetic, you lying out here all alone. Where's your family?"

Jack reached his hand out smiled as big a grin as he could muster. "I'm Jack. What's your name?"

The girl accepted the evasive answer to her question and replied, "Amy".

JEREMY NICHOLAS HERO

Chapter Two

"Well Amy, it is a pleasure. Where might you be heading?"

"I'm going all the way to Tulsa. My family is waiting for me there. I can drop you there or anywhere in between."

Jack was used to being lied to on the road. Rarely do drivers give up where they're going because they may or may not want you along for the entire trip. They typically pick a destination where they think they may become weary of the hitchers presence. It struck him that she said, "Tulsa". That was actually quite a ways to put up with a stinking straggler. They also almost always tell who is waiting for them whether or not anyone is. Jack figured this to be a defensive position as if telling him that someone was waiting at the other end of the journey would most certainly thwart any ill will from him.

He figured she was telling the truth. *Why would she pick such a distant destination just to lie about who she was meeting?* Jack sat down in the passenger seat after stuffing his bag over the headrest and letting it fall into the rear floorboard with the thud of a hobo's belongings. Amy seemed nice and a little naïve. Jack considered telling her that it wasn't safe for her to be picking random people up on the side of the road. But she had a sense of blind strength about her, like she was confident in her power however false it may be. He was attracted to it immediately. Maybe she was stronger than he believed. Maybe he was wrong altogether and she was someone even stronger than he. She certainly appeared to be in this moment. Jack sank back into the seat and switched his eyes hard to the left as he could. He wanted to look at her without her noticing.

Her legs were long and lay under the dash, occasionally bumping the tops of her thighs on the steering wheel and leaving a momentary white line across her naturally tanned legs. Farther up, she wore a simple pair of cut-off jean shorts that seemed a bit odd in November. But, this was a mild day. Jack didn't want to appear obvious. So he found a reason to turn around to get a quick glance at the rest of her. Her breasts filled out a white cotton t-shirt that read something about giving blood and her face was round and innocent with piercing eyes the color of the seas in which Jack swam as a boy when fishing in the Keys of Florida. He looked back forward quickly so as to not embarrass himself by getting caught gawking at his beautiful driver. He was struck by her and the thoughts of riding on to Tulsa entered his mind. But he could not do that. She was nice. But he was certain there was a good looking young man waiting for her in Oklahoma or waiting for her to return to whatever magical place she must have just come from.

Jack wanted desperately to get another look. But the chance would have made him obvious and so he answered her original question. "You can drop me in Willow at the Junction or if you get sick of me before then, My Hope will be fine."

"Alright, we'll see how this goes."

Jack thought to himself, *What a smart-ass!* But he loved her sarcasm. What a strange feeling he had. He had waited all this time to return to his beloved land and now wanted nothing more than to skip the whole thing and follow this girl to the ends of the

Earth and he didn't even know her. He tried to think of as many reasons to dislike her as possible. It helped a little to quash his emotions and allowed him to set himself straight as a Ranch Bound Hobo and not a Female Following Romantic. He looked around the car a little, trying to find anything wrong. There were potato chip bags in his floorboard. He thought, *Hmm, she doesn't even clean her car. She's probably just a pig, leaving trash everywhere.* Jack was looking for any way he could to not like her that he found as many petty things as he could. *Her "check engine" light is on which probably means she isn't taking care of her car. The short shorts probably indicate that she is flaunting those desirable legs for attention which must mean that there isn't a lot going on upstairs.* He somehow knew he was wrong about all of this. But, at the time, it seemed the only way to quiet his mind regarding the beautiful girl next to him.

Their conversation was sweet with a quick volley of awkward platitudes. Jack learned that she had lived in Searcy and really was heading to see family. She studied at some college, taking only part-time classes and traveling in her little red Honda as much as possible. She stayed with friends there and worked only to get enough money to go on her mini-excursions. Jack was instantly impressed. She was a traveler just like him. She certainly did it with a bit more class than Jack. But the same voice of the open road called to them and they responded much like one another. He couldn't see her riding a rail and sleeping in boxcars. He most certainly could not see her walking up lonely highways in the middle of the night, only to end up sleeping under an overpass, hungry and tired. They were very different in many ways. Yet in some ways, they were the same.

As they drove along, they passed an old rundown bar on their right. It was a stone building and the cruel Missouri weather had worn the roof to a thin layer of meager protection, barely thicker than a good stock of paper. She spoke up and said, "What about you, Jack? What makes a nice young man abandon all that he is supposed to do, to travel the road?"

"How do you know this is not what I am supposed to do?"

"Good point, my friend."

"Amy, I just enjoy this way of life. I have yet to find a lot of comfort in the grinding lives of working men and women. I do what I need to survive and I make do well enough to suit me."

"Well, I guess I cannot argue with that. Are you sure you aren't running away from something though? Are you angry at your folks? What gives, man?"

"We all got a lot to be angry about, Amy. I'd be a liar if I told you I was fine with everything around me. I just choose this life as I get up in morning. Tomorrow, I may choose to jump off the rail and go to work full-time and marry a pretty girl like you, give her babies and make her fat."

Amy giggled at the thought and Jack smiled and added, "But, probably not." As My Hope grew nearer, Jack wanted more and more to just make the ride to Tulsa Town. He knew he shouldn't. So, he replaced that with a question he was certain he already knew the answer.

"Amy, this ranch I'm gonna visit; It's a real nice place; eight hundred and fifty acres of pure paradise. I'm sure they wouldn't mind me having a visitor if you wanted come relax for a few days." Jack immediately wanted to retract his words. What was I thinking? She doesn't even know who I am! Jack beat himself up in his mind as the words poured from Amy's lips.

"That's a sweet offer, man. But I have to go see the family. Jack, what do you plan on doing with me when we get there?" Jack was stopped in his tracks. He had no idea how to answer. Was it an invitation to bring her along or was this just a cruel way to make fun of him?

Jack answered, "I don't mean anything wrong by that. I just. . ." Amy interrupted him with a burst of laughter and it angered him.

"Never mind, I'm sorry I brought it up", Jack said.

"Aww don't feel bad sweetie. It's okay."

Jack was embarrassed and wanted the car to stop. The last three miles were driven in silence and Jack could think of no way to break it. He had been caught trying to seduce this smart girl. She obviously beat him to it and now he looked like the idiot. He sat there in his shame and wondered what must be going through her mind.

Amy thought of Jack as an awkward young man. She had no fear of him and knew his boyish intentions were innocent enough. She liked him and wondered what it would be like to follow this strange young man named Jack to his ranch and spend a few days simply relaxing and playing. *No way!* She thought to herself. There was no way she would let herself be tricked into something so foolish. She had other obligations that could not be dropped for such a silly rendezvous. Her father would be forever disappointed if she were to be absent again for a family gathering just because she ran off to "chase windmills". That is what her father called it from the book, "Don Quixote" He was always running off trying to fight windmills on his beloved horse, "Rocinante".

Her father was an educated man like his daughter. That is where she was certain she must've gotten her own sharp mind from. He was grounded though and she was not. Amy read like her father did. She soaked up information and loved to challenge anyone she met. But, unlike her father, she wasn't satisfied with retaining and sharing information. She felt she had to travel to every place she read about. If she didn't have the money to get there, she found some place in America that came close so as to pretend that she had traveled to the far away land in her book.

Once, Amy read about the tall bent palm trees in Cuba. The story she read depicted a young girl lying under them and staring upward until she was dizzy with their swaying beauty. Amy had no money to reach Florida or California, much less Cuba. So she found a tall Arkansas Pine grove within twenty five miles of her home. She drove there and lay under that grove. She wore a little sun dress that reminded her of being a little girl and uttered little girl giggles as she lay under the pines. She focused only on the tall trunks of the trees and blurred out the tops. She lay there for hours imagining the tops to be the giant palm leaves and watched the trunks sway with the wind. Amy had the ability to satisfy her need to travel in this way. Although her friends, constantly made fun of her quirky adventures, she steadied her course further and paid no mind to their jeering. She was comfortable in what made her happy and never made any apology for it.

****

The little red Honda's brakes squeaked again as the Junction neared and Amy veered the small car onto the exit ramp. This was the end of their ride and Jack, ashamed of his previous remarks, was nearly one foot out the door as the car slowed to a stop at the Junction's Country Store. His head hung low, Jack thanked her for the ride and asked if he could wash her windows at the pump to repay her.

"Listen to me, Jack."

Jack raised his head and for the first time was able to look at her square on. She was beautiful. Her hair shone in the yellow sun and fell over her small shoulders as if it were placed there by the god in which Jack refused to believe. Her sea green eyes looked at him with a pity that he could not stand to witness. Jack was awe-struck and tongue tied. "What?" He said softly.

"I come back and forth this way as often as I can. Do you have a way I can get in touch with you?"

"Mind if I borrow a piece of paper and a pen?" Jack asked.

"Sure."

Amy turned around in her seat and reached behind her, shuffling through loose papers. A few seconds later, she surfaced again with a pen and a handful of crumpled receipts. "One of these oughta do, Right?" Jack took the pen and one of the receipts and wrote the address and phone number to the ranch.

"This is where I am staying. You could call me maybe one of these nights if you get bored hanging out with your family."

"I will do that. In fact, with the address, I may just stop by and see you."

"That'd be great. But ya better call first. That address will get mail. But the land is another good two miles in the middle of nowhere. Listen, Amy I didn't mean anything bad earlier..."

"Shut-up, Jack. Now, I have to get to my family and I am looking forward to running into you again one day. Let's leave it there for now."

"Not a problem." said Jack.

Jack left the car and completely forgot about his offer to wash her windows. He wondered if she just needed him gone or if she may really call. She certainly didn't offer her number to him. He thought himself a fool for getting so wrapped up in a girl during a twenty minute ride to the next major town. He had been around women before and never had too much trouble making acquaintance with them. They were typically enamored with the thought of his travels and he could make them drunk with excitement as he told stories of where he had been. If the stories didn't get their attention, he lied and made them better.

But these were stupid girls and Amy was no stupid girl. Jack feared he would never see her again. But in the same breath, he vowed that if he did, he would make the next time count.

The little red Honda skipped the pumps and drove to the top of the exit ramp. At the last moment he saw a little pretty arm covered in cheap bracelets, sticking out of the driver's side glass, waving. He raised his hand high in the air and waved back dramatically as if his hand were a large white, "I surrender" flag. She dropped over the hill and on to the highway just as quick as she approached him. His heart sank. His flag hand fell and Jack looked away from the ramp reluctantly.

CHAPTER THREE

The sun had gone low in the early November evening. The Junction had nearly become a ghost town since the last time Jack had been there. There were no semis stopping by. Only a few families in minivans and large cars that came to buy silly novelties like hillbilly backscratchers and corn cob pipes were left to roam the empty Junction parking lot and Country Store. None of these people were going to give him a ride anywhere. It is very rare, practically unheard of, for a family to pick up a hitcher. The Junction was dying. The building's bricks cracked in long horizontal lines, permanently scaring its surface as the building settled finally, never to be fixed or shored up again. The old fuel pumps were nearly completely out of commission and only two of the four operated properly. The others wore ugly handmade "Out Of Order" signs on them like ill-behaved children in a classroom. The familiar black spot painted itself on the gravel just to the north corner of the old station, peeking around at Jack. It seemed to sneak behind him nowadays. But, it wasn't real to Jack. There was a reason for these things. One time on a road trip across Georgia, Jack had been awake and riding for over forty-eight hours with a trucker that shared his "Stay Awake" pills. It surely did keep him awake. His heart slammed rapidly in his chest. His eyes were wide and darted about the dark cab of the truck. The highway lights in each passing town were only blue streaks of beauty flying by at warp speed. But on I-75, somewhere north of Atlanta, Jack watched a camel walk across the road in front of him; the effects of delirium. Surely, this was something of the sorts. Jack made himself eat a few crackers and drink some of the spring water from his canteen before walking to the next station, a big new truck stop, at the new Junction in Willow, just a mile or so north. This one had a big ramp and trucks were going through all afternoon.

However, the trucks were all going north and south by the time they got there and Jack needed to find a vehicle traveling east. He sat and waited. He couldn't get Amy off his mind. The last time he was this sick over a girl was at a KOA, ironically in Loveland, Colorado when he was only ten. His parents, grandparents and a few aunts and uncles were vacationing with his sister and him on a ski trip. They were too poor at the time to afford the big ritzy cabins. So, they saved their money to ski and play and stayed in a small Winnebago camper all piled up like Sardines in a can.

At times, tensions rose like fire among a family that loved one another dearly. The only rest that anyone got from the hard times and the arguments were to go for long walks and that is exactly where Jack met her. His father had finally had enough of the women talking bad about the women that weren't there. His mother hadn't slept well for days. His grandmother began to cry for everyone to get along and enjoy Christmas and his granddaddy had isolated himself to the cab of the camper to stay away from it all. Jack's sister had broken her leg in an accident the day before. But no one believed it was broken. They had tried to make her walk on it and she would fall down and scream in pain. By the time the second opinion came along, she had in fact, snapped her femur almost completely in half. Jack's father felt terrible about it and his sister lay there in the back of the camper in agony.

He had all he could take finally and Jack's father reached for a paper-towel roll and flung it as hard as he could against the wall, letting out a scream that could have awakened the dead. The black spot remained on the wall as the paper towel roll fell like a boulder to the thin plywood and carpet floor. Ten-year old Jack was mortified and ran out of the camper as fast as his little legs could carry him. He stopped in the white snow and fell to his knees in tears. He looked around and saw a light about a hundred yards from where he sat. Little Jack walked to the light.

About half-way there, Jack noticed her silhouette just like he was to notice Amy's, years later. She was little, like him, and crouched in the snow just as he was only minutes ago. Her hair was dusted with the soft white snowflakes that fell from the black sky. Her face was a darker complexion than Jack's Scotch-Irish heritage. She almost seemed to be some strange Colorado native that had wandered out of the mountains. Jack startled her.

"Huh?" she said. Jack was frozen with fear and didn't know what to say. This was a girl. Jack thought girls were weird and gross. But, this one was different. This one wasn't weird or gross at all. She was just scared... and pretty. She heard him walk up behind her. But, she couldn't see him in the dark. Jack was left too stupid and scared to speak. So, he coughed hard. She screamed and spun around with fury. Jack exclaimed, "Hi!" and immediately regretted his young and dumb reaction. She belted him hard across his face with her arm and Jack fell back to the snow, tears instantly filling his stinging eyes. He let out a sad wail and she immediately jumped on top of him, placing a cold wet mitten over his quivering mouth. Jack bit hard down on the mitten and the little girl swung down hard with a meaningful left to his temple.

"Shut the hell up!" she whispered. "They're going to find me!"

"What?"

"Shut up!"

Jack lay there completely incapacitated with this strong girl on top of him. These were two things he knew nothing about, a girl using the "h" word and any girl lying on top of him. He was thrilled. He just lay there soaking it all up with a gigantic grin and hoped she would never get up. But she did quickly. She looked down on him and said, "My sisters and I are playing hide and seek. Wanna play?" Little Jack said, "Hell yeah" in the best grown up cussing voice he could muster. She giggled at him and Jack felt the blood rush to his cold cheeks.

She grabbed the sleeve of his jacket and pulled him upward and off they ran into the cloudy night. Jack forgot all about his cramped up angry family in the Winnebago. He forgot all about his poor sister in pain and let the girl lead him over the boundary fence and across the road into an Aspen grove. They sat there in the shadow of the silver tree trunks and breathed heavily from the run.

"What's your name?" she asked.

"Jack."

"That's an old person name."

Jack didn't know what to say. So he said, "Yep, I don't know why they named me that".

"Your funny, you know?"

"I know. They all say that."

"Who?"

"Who what?" Jack asked.

"Who all says that?" she replied.

"I don't know. I'm confused"

Suddenly Jack heard the sisters coming near and he pulled the girl down into the snow and wrapped his arm around her to hide her all to himself. "They're coming" he said.

She said "I know. This is nice, huh?"

"Yeah."

"Wanna do it?"

"Huh? Do what?"

The girl giggled and Jack felt stupid. He knew what she meant. But he was scared. He just lay there holding on to her and she let him for a moment. Then she jumped up as soon as the sister went the other way. Jack looked at her standing over him. She wore a little blue coat that had flower shaped plastic buttons and a hood from which two long strings hung to tighten it up. Her brown hair burst toward him from under the hood and Jack was immediately in love.

They spent the next five days hiding from her sisters after Jack got home from skiing with his family. Jack never got so much as a kiss, though it wasn't for his lack of effort. That was the only night she offered him anything more than to hold her tight while they hid from the seeking sisters. Jack didn't mind though. He was content with the innocent play.

The day she left, it hurt him deeply. Jack stepped outside the creaking camper door and made a beeline to the light that was her family's RV. She was standing up in the rear glass panel looking at him between two curtains as it pulled away. She was bouncing up and down smiling and laughing as the big RV pulled out of site. Jack, again, fell to the snow in just the same position he was in when he found her. *How could she be excited to leave me? She's bouncing and giggling there in the window!* He sat there in the snow with his heart torn out in front of him. *I'll never see her again and she doesn't even care. She would rather go on her stupid trip with her stupid family and her stupid sisters that messed everything up!*

Jack sulked back to his granddaddy's little Winnebago with his angry family inside. He climbed up on the over cab bunk and lay there quietly crying to himself as the noises of dinner being made filled the musty air. Jack wanted nothing to do with dinner and ate only what they made him eat that night.

Only a few hours later, they pulled out of the camping spot and on to the cold and broken highway. The wind blew the fallen snow south across the road in gusty wisps. His father ducked to avoid the low ceiling and stepped out of the cab. He headed to the very back of the camper in order to tend to Jack's sister's broken leg. Jack climbed up front with his granddaddy. The sounds of the CB radio filled the air.

"Hey there bud, you wanna do a radio check?" Jack's granddaddy asked.

This was usually a sure thing and something Jack loved to do. He would inquire to any other truck driver out there as to whether they could hear him coming through clearly over the radio. To which they would nearly always reply that they did hear him and as long as the conversation remained appropriate for young ears, his granddaddy would let him continue the exchange for as long as he wanted.

But, this time all Jack replied was, "No sir. That's okay."

The white line of the highway flung by his window as fast as the old camper could sling it, and the radio blared with the sounds of The Chuck Wagon Gang. Jack's granddaddy wasn't the greatest consoler when it came to a young boy with a broken heart. He just pushed a pack of powdered doughnuts over into his grandson's lap and said, "Eat that. I think they're good for yeh." Jack smiled a little and took one out of the package and after three were consumed his granddaddy looked over and grabbed the package. "They aint that good for yeh! Leave some fer me, now!"

CHAPTER FOUR

Jack thought fondly of his grandfather. His memories were sweet and Jack missed him dearly. Growing up, they rarely agreed or saw eye to eye. But, he wished for the old man's guidance from time to time. Jack's grandfather was soft in heart and hard-set in his mind, which did not always flow with Jack's free spirit. However, in times of need, Jack would still call on him as if he may answer his desperate plea for help. It was futile. However, Jack felt all the better for doing it.

****

As he arrived at the new Junction, he found a curb that still retained some of the sun's warmth to sit on, and reached deep into his pack for his pen and his notebook. As things came to his mind, Jack loved to jot them down. His grandfather was on his mind tonight. Jack knew he would have to pass the time waiting for a ride and his chances were a little better as the sun went down. Someone would surely take more pity on a poor, cold soul rather than just a poor soul.

Now, to pass the time; Jack reached deep into his memory and thought of different instances, growing up. He contemplated it deeply, pulled the notebook to his blue jean lap and began writing until someone would check to see if he needed a ride.

****

My first memory of him is so very vague; I wonder how accurate it must be? I remember us walking. It was a hot South Florida day. I'm not sure what time of day. I only remember it was light out, the kind of light you experience when walking out of a matinée at two o clock in the afternoon. There was a forgiving breeze rushing through the dry, swaying palmettos and it felt like a cool clean bed sheet on the back of my neck. As we walked or jogged, as was his habit, I think I took two steps to keep up with his one. Down the long dirt driveway we went, pounding our feet into the gray sandy soil. I had to jump the ruts in the road as I came to them while he simply loped over them with ease. He was in better physical shape than most men his age and while I believe he never did, I knew he could come out ahead fist to fist with men half his age. He was no stranger to hard work and shunned anything that could have made his work easier. He believed in carrying, hauling, breaking and building with his hands, his back and his shoulders were strong, which he proudly carried the world on.

I had watched him leave out on his jogging trips and I wondered in my little mind where he was going. I had no conception of distance so I thought he probably went somewhere far away from there and I longed to follow him to the great places I imagined him to go. I was a fumbling, clumsy boy probably four years old. I thought of him as a mountain or maybe a sort of god. I could not imagine anything grander than to be him, my father's father. He was wise and strong in my eyes. I only saw his soft side as I got older. I remember he told me to quit looking at the ground and to look ahead so as to not run off into the bushes. On one side of the long driveway was his pasture and on the other was a canal which bordered the road and the train tracks that I would hunt rabbits on, later in my youth. The small shrubs and trees hung over the canal and it was dark and mysterious to me. I always liked to stay on the pasture side of the road when I walked down it. I was afraid a snake or gator may come slithering out of there and drag me away screaming. However, on this walk I wasn't, in the least, afraid of anything. I knew beyond a shadow of a doubt that whatever came out of that dark abyss and slithered through the bushes would meet a terrible end at the hand of this mighty man beside me.

I did not make it far before I ran out of breath and became tired. I half expected him to just leave me there panting for breath and go wherever he had to. Instead, he stopped and said it was time to go back. I thought to myself, "Thank God". But, I dared not say it. I wanted him to think I had many more miles in me even though I may have had only a few feet. It's amazing to me, the clarity we have as adults about past instances in our lives. He knew good and well that I was exhausted. But he allowed me my pride and humbly silenced himself from stating the obvious. This is something that many of us fathers and grandfathers should practice. We should, occasionally not correct our children and allow them their pride, even when we know they are wrong. Much of what they learn is from trial and error and I believe we can only teach them by way of being a guide. The human child is such a curious being that he will have to try out that which we tell them not to do. A child loves for his parent to believe in him. And for a child to have a sense of accomplishment, as I had that day, was very healthy for me. We turned around and walked back.

Early in life, I only saw his coarse rugged exterior. He was born and raised in the West Virginia hills. They called him their hometown boy. He was the son of a cabinet-maker and he married a farmer's daughter and loved her for life. As a boy, he learned to preach and loved to read. He would stay up late into the night after everyone was asleep reading by candlelight listening to the ghosts of relatives in the upstairs of their small home.

Jack thought of how he woke up early in the mornings and went to the sink in the bathroom. He remembered his grandfather would grab a bottle of rubbing alcohol and splash his face after shaving the tough gray stubble you could have struck a match on. The smell of the rubbing alcohol permeated every room of the house. He went directly to his barn and poured enough feed for all his cows, mixing sorghum in with oats and sweet feed. He then carried, by hand, each five gallon bucket of feed from the barn to his cattle two at a time. He did this every morning and every afternoon. When the cows would get what he called "onry" he would grab an empty bucket and swing hard down on the animals head and give a yell that made Jack want to run inside. But those animals respected him and believed that he was in control, as did Jack.

Granddaddy was a preacher. This was his true passion. He believed what he believed and it was based solely on what he considered to be fact. There was no diversion from scripture to him. It was black and white King James truth. He believed this was the righteous path and lived it as strict as anyone I've seen. I never saw him drink or smoke because his body was a temple and that temple was not his to destroy. I never heard a foul word exit his lips and I do not believe this was any struggle for him. My dad used to tell me that he and Granddaddy would leave out extra early for church. Granddaddy had a CB Radio attached to a speaker on the top of his truck. They would drive into some of the worst, mostly Hispanic, neighborhoods in Okeechobee County with my Granddaddy preaching over that intercom telling the people to come to church with them. My dad says this was pretty embarrassing at the time, as it would be for any young teen. But I must assume that it worked. Because I remember as I was growing up, we had a higher Hispanic membership in the summer than we did white members. It seemed more and more of these folks wanted to attend a church somewhere. The problem with some South Floridians as well as probably many southern towns of the time was that there was very little tolerance of the opposite race. They were looked at as free loaders, dirty and uneducated. They had too many kids. They didn't dress the way we white folks did. For this reason, their growing attendance at the church was becoming a large problem to some. My granddaddy just saw an opportunity to save souls and in doing so he made very close friends with many of them. At the same time he made very strong enemies within the church. I would like to tell you that this didn't bother him at all. But I would be lying. It broke his heart to see that so many of his brothers and sisters forgot why they were in church in the first place. They had forgotten the great mission. They had forgotten that Jesus preached to the masses, not the white masses, that he fed the hungry and healed the sick. He didn't dine with the rich people and cling tight to the healthy and well- to-do. Well, neither did Gordon Nicholas. He loved seeing those people walk through the doors and he would enjoy their presence for years to come whether the local people liked it or not. He would gain their respect to an extent that no other "white, farm-owning preacher-man" in Okeechobee had ever enjoyed.

This situation, although it would have disappointed his grandfather to know it, is exactly what set Jack on the path of new discovery for anything other than what those church people had to offer.

I can remember, after a visit, my grandparents had left our house in Tennessee to go back to Florida. I was probably fifteen or sixteen at the time and noticed Granddaddy had left his jacket. I don't know what made me go through the pockets, probably just sheer curiosity and a desire to understand the man a little more. What I found tore my adolescent heart out and fueled a hatred for organized religion that, I have to admit still smolders today. It was a folded piece of paper. I began to unfold it and read the words printed neatly. I cannot remember exactly how it was stated. But, due to my granddaddy's incessant desire to continue having the Mexicans come into the building, the deacons of the church were kicking him out. They fired him for doing what was right. They had asked him time and time again to either make his Hispanic followers dress and act the part or find a new place to worship. They complained that other people didn't want to come to the church because the Mexicans were there. They said that half of them didn't even understand what was being said. They didn't wear shoes. They didn't donate to the offering plate. They were messing up the song books and made the pews smell. The church wanted them out and they wanted them out now. He didn't conform to this rule and they pushed him out. After decades of service, they threw him aside because he wanted to preach to anyone and everyone. This sickened me. I felt I could see them for what they were. My granddaddy was upset too. But I must say he handled it much different than I. He went to Mexico.

He literally hopped in the bed of a pickup and rode with his friend Bernie and some of Bernie's family out of Florida through Mississippi, Louisiana, Texas, and crossed the border in Juarez. They were almost mugged somewhere along the way. He told the story best. They were driving up some mountain road and came across a log that was laid out in the middle. Granddaddy was going to get out and help move it when the driver of their pickup suddenly turned the truck on a dime and floored it out of there. They went back to Bernie's family's house and stayed the evening on the front porch, having been locked out for some reason unknown to me. The next morning they drove past the same spot on the same mountain road. This time, instead of a log in the road, there was a burned out car. Apparently, "banditos" had set up a trap for them along the road. If they had stopped, they would have, at best, been robbed and possibly killed.

He had to go down there and get some people interested in a new church and this wasn't going to stop him. This was to be a church that not only allowed the Mexicans to attend. This was going to be their church. They would have their own services. They would work together to bring as many "lost souls" as they could to their savior. It was truly a beautiful thing. Many times we would sit through their service and just listen. They sang so beautifully and *intently. They had a building to worship in, unmolested by the hypocrites of their former place of worship. They cared for it and never even messed up one song book.*

We all became close to our new friends. We all spent the night at the new building when the hurricanes would come through, telling ghost stories and listening to music. We spent many Sunday afternoons going to their homes and eating with them. We young boys would go out to the hog pens and wrestle them, of course in our Sunday clothes, trying to be the one who could hold on to the pig the longest. We would come in and have homemade tamales. I can remember thinking those old white winter birds at that church, I hated so much are probably not having near the fun I am. Winter Birds are people that only live in Florida during the winter.

The day my grandfather died is a day I will never forget. I never let the speedometer drop below eighty-five once I hit the turnpike and when I pulled into the parking lot of the hospital, my dad was there waiting on me.

He looked different to me. He wore his loss on his face which is a rare thing to see in my dad, and it was not for lack of trying to hide it. He made a valiant effort as he always does, to hide his pain in order that others may express theirs. But this time, I could see clearly that my own father had lost his own father and we both were aware that each of us was hurting deeply. His face was a little whiter and his stature a bit more feeble. I knew at that moment that I would have to do this with my own dad one day and while I had thought of it before, it was at this time that I truly felt little to no fear of that day. I saw what a man my dad was being and knew that one day; I would have to fill those shoes.

He hugged me and led me to an upper floor of the hospital to be present as my grandmother made the decision to remove her husband of over fifty years from life support. I imagined all the memories they had made and could only imagine all the thoughts that were going on in her mind. I thought of all the time they must have spent together. I thought of how she must be remembering herself and him planning and making a life and a family together. I thought... "And this is what it comes to, an abrupt end in the cycle of life. You wake up and your whole life is behind you." She built her every dream and loving thought around that man and he was gone in an instant. He was a huge, concrete, unmovable part of each of our existence and in one morning, the cornerstone of our family was shaken and forever broke. But like an old home that has settled and cracked, my family has some real character and we sent Granddaddy to God the way he would have wanted. We all stood around him with our hands on him and as he took his last breaths of air, we each took turns telling him what a wonderful man he was. We told him how much we loved him and for the first time in my life, I watched and felt life leave a human body. I had seen several people pass. But this time I actually was present and touching the person I loved as they passed on. I will never forget what an honor it was to be in that room with my granddaddy.

CHAPTER FIVE

"Hey Boy, you need a ride!"

The voice broke Jack's daydream like shattering glass. Jack swung around, instantly irritated. His notebook slid off his lap and fell to the cooling pavement. The night had long since fallen around him and he suddenly noticed the chill. The screaming man was sitting in a pick-up truck only about forty yards away, lit up only by the florescent over-head station lights. The pick-up was an old blue Ford and the man fit the truck well. He was a large frame man in a pair of dark blue-jean overalls with a black shirt that Jack couldn't read because of the front flap of the overalls. He carried around a large beer belly and wore and thick red beard that happened haphazardly all about his face. His hair matched his beard and Jack thought he seemed to appear friendly enough.

"Yes sir, if you're going east!" Jack said. This may be his only shot at not having a twenty mile walk ahead of him. So, Jack figured he better cheer up.

"Get own in, boy. I'm headin' as far as The Bluff. I can drop ya there."

"Just get me to Lucky's at Birch Creek and we're good. How 'bout that?"

"Sounds like a plan. You comin' 'er not?"

Jack smiled, picked up his notebook and shoved it and the pen back into the pack. He heaved it onto his shoulder walked toward the old blue Ford. Jack slung his pack over the bed and turned to the friendly giant. He asked the man, "back or front?" just out of courtesy.

The big man said, "Well ya might as well hop up here with me. But, I'll let ya know I'm packin'. So, don't be tryin' nothin' silly."

"You won't hear a peep outa' me, sir", said Jack.

Jack climbed in. The old Ford smelled of bad two cycle gas mix, fresh cut cedar, and beer. Just as he noticed the sweet stench of the alcohol, a cold Milwaukee's Best flew from the other end of the cab directly into Jack's lap. "Wanna beer?" Jack obliged the big man and introduced himself properly, shaking his gigantic right palm. The big man introduced himself as Farron.

The truck fired up loud with a back-fire and jolted into gear. Jack thought about asking Farron how much he'd had to drink that evening; but it seemed rude. So he refrained and prayed that Farron could drink and drive as well as most of the old hillbillies in these parts can.

They pulled out onto the big highway and started making their way south to get on the eastward ramp. It had only been a mile and Farron had already thrown one beer into the bed of the old Ford and popped open another one. He almost missed the exit and Jack kept quiet as to keep his new friend happy. Farron veered hard into the exit lane at the last minute with a small screech of the tires. Jack sunk a little in his seat and held tight to the beer between his legs. He thought to himself, *this may not have been such a great idea.*

Farron swerved all over the highway for the next twenty miles, increasing his speed to eighty when a good song came on and slowing down to fifty miles an hour for sad songs such as Patsy Cline's "I Fall To Pieces". The sad songs made the big man's eyes well up as he sang along. His voice was as terrible as his driving and Jack thought seriously about asking Farron to let him drive several times. But to insult your only ride could easily get you walking. Furthermore, when your ride is drunk and armed, you simply may never walk again. Jack kept his mouth shut and laughed when Farron did and patted his new pal on the shoulder when he sang sad.

"Hur dat lownsum wipperwill. She found a new. It flies." Farron was back to singing. Jack tried to sing along. But it was hopeless. He looked forward at the road. Blue lights were flashing ahead and Jack prayed it was a road block. Farron would get a DUI and be hauled off and Jack could simply walk the next few miles to Lucky's and wait 'til morning to call Eli for a ride. There was no such luck though. They blew by the flashing lights like lightning. Jack didn't even think Farron saw them. The cop had a little car pulled over and was searching it. There was no way he even noticed Jack's new drunk buddy. Even if he did, it appeared he had bigger fish to fry at the moment.

In a few more miles, Jack saw the little dim-lit town of Birch Creek ahead and was ever so thankful.

"Alright buddy, I appreciate the trouble. You can drop me on the next gas station to your left." Jack pleaded to anything, the man would agree.

"Naw, I'll go ahead and run ya to your place, Bub!"

"It's okay, Farron. You can drop me there and they'll come get me directly."

"Bull! I wanna see this place!"

Jack was thoroughly irritated. "Well, throw me another one of those beers and hang a left at the flashing light". Farron did so and took the left. Jack rolled his window down to get the fresh air. Farron stomped the pedal and the truck lunged forward spilling Farron's beer all over his own lap. He let out a slew of slurred profanities and ended his tirade with a loud burst of laughter.

Jack finally asked, "You want me to get us there?" The reaction was what he feared it would be.

"I been drivin' this ol' beater all over the worl'! I can run a few miles a' dirt!"

Jack said, "The road will fork up here and you're gonna wanna stay to the left."

"I hear ya, loud and peachy!"

Jack shook his head and tried to stay calm as he directed Farron and Farron's drunken truck to the entry gate of the ranch. By the time they arrived, it was eleven o' clock in the evening and the moon was high in the big Missouri sky. Farron had passed out while trying to turn the big truck around and Jack made sure it was in park and leaned Farron over the seat so he could get a little rest. Jack knew he would have to get up early to make sure Farron didn't wake up and tear through the barns and fences trying to get out of this place as he would surely have no clue as to how he arrived. He shut the door and grabbed his things out of the back as Farron started to snore like a hibernating bear.

He had finally made it to his promised land. The moon shone. But its' light failed to hide the billions of stars in the sky. The air was crisp and clean and the sound of the highway was far enough away to not be heard. Usually the night contained sounds of pond frogs, crickets, hoot owls and such. But the silence was deafening. Jack chalked it up to the time of year. *Nothing is moving in this cold but the deer. And they are too quiet to hear*, Jack thought.

Jack grabbed his pack and walked up the steps to the Blue House, situated on the south end of the property by the front gate. He tried the door. But it was locked. So, he pulled his sleeping bag off the pack and stretched it out on the porch. Jack crawled inside and listened intently for any recognizable sound. All he could hear was the lonesome wind through the trees.

CHAPTER SIX

Jack awoke well before the sun. He figured it must be about four o'clock in the morning. It was cold and the night sky, clear. There were still a billion stars in the sky. He lay there on the cold front porch of the Blue House wrapped in his sleeping bag, his arms clenched around his torso in an attempt to retain as much of his body heat as possible. Jack really wished now that the door to the little house wasn't locked and bolted. Jack would not have hesitated to step in and make a fire to warm up by. Eli wouldn't have cared. But in truth, Jack was exhausted by the time his wild ride ended the night before. Jack listened again, to hear the different early morning sounds that only the graveyard shifts, hunters, fishermen and hobos get to hear. He wanted to pick them apart and identify each one. Jack had learned to do this after a few years of living on his own. He used all of his senses and, much like the Colorado prairie dog; he listened to what surrounded him long before sticking his head out of the proverbial hole. *Wait a second! Where's Farron? Why don't I hear him snoring still?*

Jack popped up off the porch in a standing position as fast as he could. He feared Farron may have woken up in a drunken stupor and left the ranch in a fury out of pure confusion, taking a whole fence row and a few fruit trees with him. *What a welcome I won't get if he destroyed the place they loved so much in the first night.*

Jack peered forward and let his eyes adjust. *Whew! Okay, there's the truck.* Jack took a breath and headed toward it to wake Farron up and get him gone before Eli came up to greet him.

Approaching from the driver's side, Jack witnessed the big man still slumped over across the seat. His big beer belly hung naked out from the side of his overalls and the man looked terribly uncomfortable in his awkward position. The gun he had referred to the evening before was lying on the seat sticking out from under Farron's big left leg. It was an automatic pistol. Jack guessed it to be a .380. It shone bright in the seat and Jack thought it best to get it in his own hand just in case Farron was scared or confused when he woke him. Jack ever so gently placed a grip around the handle of the pistol and counted to three. *One... Two... Three.* Jack jerked the gun back quick toward him and Farron came to life.

"Wha... Huh... What the..."

"Farron, it's me Jack."

"Who? Where the hell? Who? What?"

Farron was obviously confused and hung over. Jack hid the pistol, sticking it barrel first in the seat of his pats and resting the grip over his belt. He pulled his shirt over it and squatted next to the truck. Farron sat up and inquired as to where he was. "Farron you gave me a ride here last night and passed out." Jack said. "I just let you sleep it off and now you can get on to The Bluff.

"Who said anything about The Bluff?"

"That's where you told me you were going last night."

"I did? Oh yeah, I guess I did, huh."

Jack just gave a smile and Farron apologized for his behavior. Jack assured him that he was grateful for the ride no matter how exciting the trip; Farron sat straight in his seat and rubbed his face and head in an attempt to straighten the matted wild red hair that was now, quite the sight to see. Jack wanted to ask where he was going. He wanted to find the most polite way to make sure Farron understood that Jack intended on traveling alone and didn't know what Farron's intentions were.

"Boy, I've made a mess of myself, huh."

"It's alright, Farron. Say, man, where is home if it is not The Bluff?"

"Good question, boy. My home's a wreck right now. My boy got himself killed last year and the wife and me can't seem to get it together." Farron's head sunk low and the big man seemed to shrink a bit. Jack felt somewhat at a loss for words and stood up putting his hands in his jean pockets as if the answer was somehow in there somewhere.

"I'm sorry, boy. You don't need to hear all my troubles. I appreciate ya askin' though. I figure I better be on my way."

"Farron, do you have any more kids or just the one?"

"I got another 'un. She's been angry at me for not holdin' it together for her mamma and her ever since. Don't ever lose your kids if ya got any, boy. You'll just end up lookin' like me."

"Farron, you seem like a good enough fella. You just gotta get back up on your feet. That's all."

"Easier said than done, boy."

Jack stood in the silence of the morning and Farron let out a deep breath and reached behind him. When he found nothing there, he looked bewildered and Jack remembered that he had Farron's pistol in his belt.

"I picked it up 'cause I didn't know how you'd react not knowing where you were this morning."

"Thanks, boy."

Jack reached carefully around his back and retrieved the .380. He held the barrel and extended the grip toward Farron to give the man's gun back to him. Farron reached out and took the gun from Jack, holding it against the steering wheel with the barrel pointed upward toward the windshield. Farron leaned forward and hung his head low. He sighed deeply and began to cry. Jack let Farron cry, mostly for lack of knowing any other thing to do. He wasn't comfortable with the big man holding the gun. Something felt wrong. But it was Farron's gun and Jack couldn't wrestle it away from him at this point anyway. Jack stepped back from the truck and just as he was about to think of something else to say, Farron extended the gun, butt first out of the truck and said, "Take it boy. Get it away from me."

"Farron, it's your gun, man. What would I do with it?"

"Boy take the gun or you're gonna have a hell of a mess to clean up out here!" Farron yelled.

Jack took the gun and told Farron "Buddy, I don't like the way you're talking. Can I get you some help?"

"There aint no help for me, boy. I'm a lost cause. I'm all screwed up, boy!"

Jack didn't know what to say and before he could think of anything, Farron slammed the door to the old truck and started it up. "Farron, Stop!" Jack exclaimed. But it was to no avail. Farron was intent on getting out of there. His face was white. All the blood had rushed from it. He stared blankly through Jack and said,

"Thanks for the company, boy. I'm sorry you had to meet me." Jack's heart sank for the big man and Farron spun dust up leaving the ranch gates. He went over the hill, into the darkness, and Jack stood alone with Farron's gun still in hand. For a minute or two, he listened to the big truck's tires crunch the cold gravel, heading back to the highway and Birch Creek.

****

The breeze crept into Jack's coat and across the back of his neck. He should be thrilled to be here. He should be making plans for all the adventures he would take. He was happy to be at the place he loved. But something in the air was sickening. He wondered if Farron had ruined this adventure for him and then felt angry, like maybe that is exactly what happened. But Jack knew better. Jack knew beyond a doubt that this place was as lovely as ever and that this incident with Farron created tension for him and would pass. He worried about Farron. *Would he just go get another gun and finish what seemed to be an obvious desire to end his own life?* Jack hoped that wasn't the case and that Farron had just turned a new leaf and was heading home to make things right with his family. He wondered what it must be like to raise a son, only to have all of your joy ripped away with an untimely death of somebody that you so very much loved. It didn't seem fair to Jack. In fact he knew it couldn't be fair. It was a travesty.

I hope I get to see him again. What a strange trip this seemed to be turning into. First I fell in love which led to the terrifying ride with Farron only to end up with a .380 pistol with which a man just seriously contemplated suicide. He thought of turning around and walking the six miles of dirt back to the highway and catching rides with his friends in New Orleans. *No!* Jack thought. *I am a man of my word and will do no such thing.*

The sun peeked over the eastern hillside and brought with it some warmth to Jack's heart. He stood in the same place with the .380 still at his side. *What am I gonna do with this?* He thought. He slid the cylinder out and saw that it had one shell in it. He thought that to be terribly eerie and removed it, placing it in his pocket. He turned and walked back to the Blue House, untied his pack and shoved the pistol deep inside the pile of his belongings. Eli didn't much care for guns and Jack didn't want to offend him. He, himself liked them. But he always considered it to be a bulky heavy item that would get in a hobo's way long before it would ever help him.

Jack hadn't slept well at all and wanted coffee. He wondered if Eli would be awake and might let him into Janice's home to make a fresh pot. Janice is Eli's former wife. She is a pleasant, sweet woman, still attractive in her later adult years and still full of ambition and life. Jack understood why they had divorced when they did and he admired them for being able to continue living on this beautiful land together. Janice lived in what is commonly called the Main House. It is a tri-level log home set into the side of a south-facing hill-side. Janice loves color and atop the Main House, she had a large Turquois roof installed. It was a bit odd looking. But it was colorful and beautiful, much like Janice, herself. She often looked at Jack with perplexity, as if she were asking herself, *How can such a sweet young man be so lost?* When she looked at Jack, he felt she was sorry for him in many ways. But he never defended himself because he always felt she loved him regardless. Janice hated some of the things Jack loved to do. Hunting and fishing were passions of his that Janice despised; she never let anyone hunt the land although people had asked her to and even offered her money for seasonal hunting rights. She emphatically returned their request with a solid, "No".

This wasn't the case for Jack, though. He was allowed to hunt and fish as long as Janice could remain oblivious. Anything killed in her woods was cleaned there as well. There were no trophy pictures taken and the meat was stored outside of her home. Jack rarely hunted. But, to know that he could was an honor that he dared not receive lightly. Nor did he share this with very many at all. He was certain that there were a few others that Janice bestowed this privilege upon. However, they respected the same silence and reverence about the honor as he did.

Many times, Janice would meet Jack coming up the driveway with open arms and a great smile. But if he did not see her, he always went to Eli first. She was a private woman and if she did not come out of her home, there was a reason, and Jack respected that. It took him months, the first time he stayed at the ranch, to learn the boundaries of the people there. The boundaries were invisible and appeared to not exist. However, Jack realized now that they were very real and understood that the people there, like Janice, wanted to develop a close enough relationship with people that boundaries and limits were understood without having to be put out on their sleeves.

Jack reached down and picked his pack up and slung it over his right shoulder. He stepped off the porch and looked back at the Blue House. It was a small one story cabin that had a loft in it. Windows surround the loft and the entire structure, save the foundation was painted bright blue. The foundation was made of Missouri field rock and an old sand cement mix. The family that lived here first was Mormon and had several beautiful daughters. The daughters are the ones that built the Blue House. Jack assumed that Eli painted it blue as that was his favorite color. But he wasn't sure. It was a rickety old cabin. But on winter nights, if you put a fire in both stoves, it was a beautiful sight to sit in the loft, comfortable and warm, looking out over the snow covered Ozark hill-sides under the light of the bright January moon. That was the highest point that one was able to view from inside a warm, cozy room. However, the summer was excruciating at the Blue House. There was no air conditioning and the upstairs windows turned the whole house into an oven and you could only bear to stay in it at night after it cooled down.

Turning around and facing the long quarter mile gravel drive that led to the Main House and the Bunkhouse, Jack began to walk north. The breeze still blew, stinging his eyes as he made his way down the drive. He passed the old blue barns and Shondo, a paint horse that he loved dearly. Jack had helped Eli paint the barns the last time he was here and it looked as if his work was holding up well. It was almost entirely downhill until the last leg of the driveway, and Jack's feet plopped hard on the ground in front of him. By the time he arrived at the valley, where he would begin his ascending trudge to his much missed friends, Jack noticed the first bit of purple and yellow in the sky. It was becoming daylight. Farron was more in the back of his mind and Jack only hoped Amy was enjoying her family. He did not want her all to himself now. He was beginning to get excited about his visit. The birds were singing loudly. The wind could be heard coming over the hills and the last dying leaves rattled in the trees.

A light shone from the second story of the Main House and Jack hope Janice would come and say hello soon. He would love to see her. But he would equally appreciate a hot cup of coffee. His wish came true as he neared the entrance of the mud room. The door swung open and Janice laughed loudly, welcoming him with a hug. It was so sweet to be home. She looked very well and happy. Jack's heart sang with excitement.

"I had a feeling you were close last night!" said Janice

"I was. I stayed at the Blue House so as to not wake anyone with my late arrival."

"It's locked, silly! How did you get in?"

"I stayed on the porch last night and I don't want any grief over it. The stars were beautiful." Jack said with a grin.

"Well you should have just knocked and I would have put you on a couch."

"I know. I know. Hey, you wouldn't have a little coffee would ya?"

"C'mon in."

Jack followed Janice into the Main House, careful to remove his shoes. Janice boiled water as Jack sat down at the kitchen bar and took the cozy familiar place in. The fire in the stove crackled and only an over-head light was on. The room was dimly lit with the first light of the morning beginning to pour in from the large picture windows looking out over the valley and up toward the Blue House. They made small talk about where Jack had been the last year and the goings on of the ranch.

"The trail to the river has overgrown quite a lot and Eli will need some help cutting firewood, if you feel up to it," said Janice Jack excitedly agreed. This is why he came. He loved the work because it placed him outside in his natural element. He enjoyed the risk and the sweat, the occasional scrape and cut. It was as if the land was his own and that thinking was encouraged by his family here.

The kettle screamed like the horn of a steam engine, indicating that the water was boiling heavily. Janice removed it from the eye of the stove and poured it gently into the glass cylinder of the French press. Janice plunged and pressed the coffee grounds to the bottom until all that was left in the cylinder was the hot black coffee that Jack was longing for to kick-start his new day. Janice poured his cup and then her own. The coffee was strong, just the way he liked it, and it took effect quickly. Jack was ready to get out and see the land. He was ready to see the river and cut the firewood.

Janice looked at him and said, "Jack, how long do you plan on staying this time?"

"I'd like to get through the winter, Janice, if that's alright."

"Oh, of course it is, sweetie."

Jack noticed some hesitation in her words or something like her mind may be wandering. Yes, that was it. Janice's mind wandered somewhere just then. Something was wrong. She seemed burdened and worried.

Jack interjected, "Hey Janice, if you guys are wanting a little less company this winter, I could stay up at the Blue House or I could visit for a week or two and keep moving. I certainly don't want to be a burden."

"Absolutely not!" she said with a smile. "You'll stay where you want, Jack and as long as you want."

Jack still sensed a tension and he didn't know where it was coming from or what it was. Janice definitely seemed a little strange and distant. Her imploring his presence, at will, wasn't genuine and Jack knew it. Jack poured another cup of coffee as Janice stared out the window toward the cold valley. It fell silent in the house and Jack searched the room for something to speak of to break the uncomfortable silence. What could he think of to say?

"I met a girl on the way here. She gave me a ride and she may call one of these evenings for me. Her name is Amy, if she does call."

"She gonna be staying here too?" replied Janice, coldly with contempt in her voice.

That settled it. Something was very different. Eli and Janice had always welcomed him. It was too early in the winter for cabin fever. The days were still nice, no matter how cold the night. Jack was hurt and shocked by her comment and immediately regretted his decision to come here. *Had Janice not been aware of my coming?* He wondered. He had told Eli by phone, months ago and Eli seemed excited and happy to hear that he was going to spend time here and help.

"Jack answered her question as best he could, "I don't think so, Janice. Hey what's going on? I really feel like I am intruding."

Janice sighed and laid her head down on the bar. Jack pushed the issue more and Janice would not respond. She only sat there, head down and refusing to look up and answer him. Jack stood up and said, "Janice, I am going to take a walk and leave you be for little. I'd like to come back and talk in bit if that would be alright." Janice continued to not respond.

Jack turned and left the Main House and headed past the bunkhouse to his right when he saw Eli in the semi-outdoor kitchen. He appeared to be reading a book. Jack approached the threshold and gave a sharp knock to the flimsy screen door. Eli turned and slowly stood up. Eli stood almost a full foot taller than Jack. He was strong and thin, keeping a one week growth of facial hair and a head full of the grey hair that he only combed for special occasions, of which Jack remembered many, even out here in the woods. Eli was not unclean or un-hygienic. He just didn't concern himself with a perfect hairdo when his days were filled with hard work in the rocky Ozark hills. He ambled over to the door and pushed it open.

"Come on in." Jack stepped in the door. The kitchen was awry. There were pots and pans stacked upon one another, all over the place. The floor was covered in mud that had been tracked from the outside. It smelled of rotting food and mildew. Jack was again thrown back by the shape in which Eli had left the outdoor kitchen. It was usually clean and well kept. It was important to because it was more exposed to animals and nature than any other kitchen on the land. Jack also had helped Eli build this structure. They worked hard, from early morning until late in the evening laying huge rocks and poring homemade cement. The original idea for the building was an outdoor kitchen which is why Jack still terms it as that. However, once Eli and Jack completed it as an outdoor kitchen, Eli came into some large glass panels. He decided he wanted to close in the building with glass and screens.

Back to work they went, day and night, laughing and sometimes cursing as they went along. It was delightful work. None of Eli's construction projects ever really had a beginning or an end. They would start by accident and then Jack would hear him say something that sounded much like an excited, ambitious man, part construction worker and part mad scientist.

"Jesus Mary and Baby Jesus, Jack! Get me a hammer!"

As the work went along from there, the project always grew into something else. The buildings became dual or multi-purpose. Eli's tree house became his garage. The kitchen had a bath-house attached. The bunkhouse ended up with a loft apartment and an open air workout room that overlooked an amphitheater with a stage.

But, again this wasn't the Eli that he remembered. His face was ashen and forlorn. Jack could not see his eyes for the way Eli seemed to keep them turned down and away. His tall handsome frame was a little bent and there was no excitement in him, no ambition. The entire place felt lifeless and Jack was finally in front of the man that he was absolutely free to speak in any way he wished. With Janice, he was more reserved. But Eli was not just a teacher and host to Jack. Eli was simply one of Jack's best friends.

"Eli, what the hell is going on here? What is wrong with everyone?"

Eli turned around slowly and made his way back to the table. As he sat, Jack expected that he just needed a few moments to gather a way to tell Jack some terrible news. So, he was patient and followed Eli and sat at the table with him. Eli sighed and put his head down low, much like Janice did moments ago. Jack continued to wait patiently. But Eli gave no answer. So, Jack decided a little more forwardness was in order.

"Eli, the kitchen looks like hell. You don't look much better. The same thing is wrong with Janice. I want to know what it is right now. Nobody is telling me anything! I want to know!"

Eli didn't budge.

"Eli, I want to know!" Jack said loudly. But, still there was no result. Jack stood up and walked around the table slowly placing his hand his old friends shoulder. "Eli..."

Eli swung his head around with a quick twist and glared at Jack through a pair of empty hateful eyes. "You already know!" he screamed

Jack jumped backward and reeled in disbelief that his friend would yell at him like this. His jaw open, he just stared at Eli and a tear welled in his eye. Here, his best teacher and friend sat, crumpled in a chair. His powerful ally had been broken by something fierce and Jack couldn't begin to put a finger on it. Nor was Eli appearing to want to speak of it. Jack knew within his soul that something was deeply wrong. This was not the culmination of a few bad days or cabin fever. This was completely out of character for both Eli and Janice. Jack felt a sudden fear grip him. He felt dizzy. He tried to shake it. He attempted to think of any way out. *Is this a nightmare? Am I still sleeping at the Blue House?* He asked himself every question he could think to rationalize what was happening in front of him. But none of it added up. None of it boiled down to this. Yet this was really happening.

Jack backed up away from Eli and stood still, observing the stranger in the chair. Eli wore his signature blue jeans and white t-shirt. On his feet were the same sneakers that didn't fit a man working in the woods. They more fit a basketball player. But the Eli he knew cared more about being comfortable than anything, and this was how he was most comfortable. The difference physically however, was astounding. His usual strong posture was replaced with a slouch that he had never displayed along with being bent at the back and having his head hung low. He was pale and his hair, although the usual gray, was a little whiter. The eyes were something Jack had never seen. Eli was intelligent, wise beyond many men he knew and his eyes reflected that calm, friendly wisdom. These were not his eyes. It seemed something evil had possessed his soul and traded his kind eyes for something demonic, full of hate and contempt. Physically though, he did not appear hateful and mean. He appeared to be thoroughly broken, destroyed by a burden that was unidentifiable to Jack.

For now, I'll have to leave him be and figure this thing out, thought Jack. He knelt next to Eli and looked up into his face. "I don't know what has got a hold of you and Janice. But I am here to help. I'm going to get this fixed, Eli."

His words brought a redness to the hateful eyes and tear fell from his dear friend's ashen cheek to the wood top table and soaked its salty body into it. Eli refrained from any response and it appeared the tear was not willing. It had been choked from him.

Jack thought to himself, *If the tear was so unwilling, why is my friend holding this in? Eli had never held anything in. If he felt it, he said it. What were the consequences of talking about it? Why couldn't Eli talk?*

CHAPTER SEVEN

Jack stepped out into the cool morning. The sun had given way to clouds forming in the western sky, heading towards him. His hopes for returning to this place seemed dashed to a million pieces. The clouds seemed as if they were looming overhead with the ominous warning to leave this place and forget all about it. The ranch was twisted and wrong. Everything around him seemed to wear a hue of sadness and neglect. He listened intently. But, he could make out no sound save the same wind rattling the same dead leaves high in the tall oaks that shrouded the giant forest between Jack and the river.

He wondered who else was here. Surely, there was someone other than Eli and Janice present that could explain a little about what was happening here. Jack felt a responsibility to this land and could not allow it to remain barren, desolate and sad. He turned to the bunkhouse. The windows were dark and gray with dust that had settled from the inside. There was very little fire wood stacked out front which was odd this time of year.

He trotted down to the front door and pushed the heavy thing open. It was black inside and the silence in the old building sucked Jack through the door, although he should have thought better about entering such a hole. He thumbed the switch on the wall and nothing happened. *The fuse box may be shut off for lack of use,* he thought. There was a nine volt yellow flashlight sitting in the window. Jacked flipped it on and the room lit up. The light exposed a forgotten, abandoned room. The floor was covered in bark from firewood that had been hauled in last winter. Papers were strewn about the floor and being blown around by the wind that entered a broken window on the south facing side. Jack moved forward a little and there sat a desk to his left, the chair next to it toppled over and was left to lay there by someone who must've been in a hurry to leave. A sleeping bag lay crumpled up in the corner. The pillow was thrown across the room to the other side. Candles lay upright and only a quarter or so of their life had been melted away. Jack felt as if he was playing a game of detective.

He figured the desk, the crumpled sleeping bags, and the pillow were clues that someone bolted out of here quite some time ago. However the candles not being burned completely out indicated that either, one: they took time to blow them out, two: they left quickly during the day when they weren't being used or three: the person here was lazy and didn't clean up their mess. The latter was unlikely because even the messiest irresponsible idiots that bedded down at the ranch for any amount of time were encouraged regularly to not leave a mess. Often, people stayed for free in exchange for work, and the last thing most people would want would be to destroy or damage that relationship over a mess left behind. So, Jack thought, it had to be one of the first two.

Making his way on through the bunkhouse, Jack pushed on the back door of the main room. It appeared to be stuck. He pushed harder and it budged a bit. But it would not open. Jack considered kicking it. He thought better of it. *If this is all a misunderstanding, I'll certainly look crazy going around kicking doors open.* He backed up and looked at it, perplexed. The room behind the door was a small bedroom that could be used by a couple that may not want to sleep in a room full of people or a female that may be sharing the bunkhouse with a group of men. It was just a small privacy room. There was another entrance from the other side. As Jack thought about simply going around the outside and trying the other door, he took one more step back and he backed directly in to a person. He lunged forward toward the door and spun in one motion only to see Janice standing behind him. She stood there staring blankly through him, her pretty hair disheveled and her arms outstretched toward Jack. She had a helpless look of desperation plastered on her face. She stood there frozen. Jack screamed and covered his face with his arms.

"Janice! What the hell!" Jack slowly lowered his arms from a defensive position and looked back to where she was. She stood, now with her hands to her side; although her hair was the same and her face forlorn, she no longer wore the look of utter desperation.

"Get out of here. This is private," she said.

"Janice, please tell me what is going on here. Something is wrong and you have to tell me what it is. Let me help, Janice. I love you and Eli both. Please let me help. Just tell me what is wrong!" Janice almost giggled and contemptuously replied, "You already know."

"That's not gonna cut it! I wouldn't ask if I didn't know. What the hell is it Janice!"

"You already know!" she screamed with her hands over her eyes as if looking at him was revolting.

She turned her back to Jack and went to one of the north windows just past the desk, stepping carelessly all over the papers on the floor. She stared through it, looking into the rattling oaks that continued their horrible sound. Jack asked her, "Who else is here?"

"Who else has ever been here Jack, but you?"

"Where are they Janice?"

"You... killed him. Look at us, Jack."

She gave no other answer he could hear. She took a long breath and sighed a whisper that Jack could not comprehend. Jack moved behind her and tried to see what her eyes were fixed upon out there in the woods. He could see nothing but what had always been there. Jack didn't want to leave her in the bunkhouse.

"Janice, please step outside with me."

She gave no response. Jack left her inside and began making his way to the front door. As he approached it, he felt the longing to turn around and get another glimpse of his dear friend. When he did, he could see to the back of the bunkhouse where he stood only moments ago. The closed door that he had pushed on so diligently stood as open as it could get; and the room was black as midnight.

"You did it again, didn't you, Jack?"

Jack stepped out the door and found his pack lying outside the outdoor kitchen. He rummaged through it and found his tobacco and papers. His fingers trembled as he tried to roll the cigarette. He managed the task after tearing only one paper. Eli still sat at the table, now reading nothing, simply staring at the grains in the wood top, bent in the same awkward position. Jack lit the quivering rolled paper in his lips and drew hard, finding a stump to sit down on. He inhaled the smoke and let it roll out as he tried to make some sense of what was going on. He considered calling the sheriff to come out and check on them. *But what would the sheriff say? What would my story be? 'Two weird people are living in the woods almost completely off the land and they are acting strange'."* Jack doubted that would warrant much attention from law enforcement. Furthermore, if this was something that Eli and Janice could snap out of, they would never forgive him for calling the law to their land. He wondered what he could do and the only solution that felt right was to stay here and figure out what must be done to fix it all.

When Jack stayed here before, he often played the role of a protector, a warrior against things that may harm these sweet people that only wished to live in peace, by themselves. Jack could often be found running poachers off the land or fixing a car that had something simple wrong with it. He often tended fires, cut wood, removed unwanted pests such as snakes and skunks and occasionally did the dirty deeds of putting an animal down to end its suffering; breaking a horse to ride, and protecting the integrity of the land itself by keeping unwanted and harmful people away, sometimes with a ferocious spirit when talking failed to send the message. He was protector of this land and that burden was one that Jack carried with pride.

It was time for him to wear that crown of thorns again. It was his job to keep this place safe and he had done well with it when he was here before. These people were different. They wanted to live a certain way. Jack was a peaceful, respectable way for them to achieve that, and not have to deal with the things that made them uncomfortable, because they could call on him to fix it. *Was that it? Is that why things are the way they are now? Have I neglected this place to the point that everyone has left and Eli and Janice have gone crazy?*

Jack thought better of it but left it as a possibility in his mind, however egocentric it was. It did give him a drive. He thought, *maybe a bit of ego couldn't hurt my chances at helping Eli and Janice come back to reality.*

Jack stood with his new conviction set firmly in his mind and decided the first order of business was to find out if anyone else was here. First, he headed back toward Eli's tree house. He walked down the dirt path eastward past the old medicine wheel and the remnants of a sweat lodge that had been burned. It did not smolder. The willow ashes still, somewhat held their original form. The altar bore precious offerings, not yet windblown or faded by the sun. It had been burned recently. Jack knew that lodges are rarely burned. Usually it requires tragedy. Something awful has happened. As he walked he remembered the last burning lodge. He remembered the tears that poured from the stinging eyes of his loved ones as they stood around it and watched the flames engulf the twisted willow branch frame. He could he hear his wailing ancestors accept the offering and mourn the loss of such a beautiful space, a space that had been used for purposes of peace and positive intentions.

He remembered the first time he had sat in the lodge, the strange acclimation to this world that he had no knowledge of until it was revealed to him by his teachers, Eli and Brody.

****

Jack came to the ranch for the first time when he was eighteen years old with a group of friends that used the land as a retreat place. They were basically a group of likeminded friends that were seeking to understand love and worshipped the idea of being able to love unconditionally. They studied this form of love and tried to practice it among themselves with the goal of being able to live by it as closely as possible. The ranch was a wonderful place for them to have a retreat because it was secluded, for the most part, from all the negative influences of a world that rarely practiced anything without conditions. Jack's small group of friends would meet up with people from all over the country and spend a three-day weekend in the Ozarks; and it was absolute bliss.

Jack's teacher at the time was a man by the name of Brody. Brody was the one who that talked Jack into attending this weekend seminar of sorts. He was about five foot ten and probably weighed one hundred and forty pounds, soaking wet. Brody was about fifty years old or so, and gave very sound advice. He had three bloodhounds and an old cat that passed away during a gathering of friends, one night. Jack thought he would never get over that. Brody's animals were more than pets. They were his family, his children. He lived alone and these were all he had aside from his friends. Brody didn't talk much nonsense, either. He was sort of a loner and that is one reason why Jack liked him so much. Jack always appealed to loners as they did to him, however ironic that may be.

Jack could still hear his wise friend's words today;

"Jack you should attend this retreat. I've helped you about as much as I can. There is a man that you need to meet; this man named Eli."

"Brody, man, I am comfortable with you. You know me better than anyone!"

"Jack, you are heading in a direction of which Eli is more capable of teaching you than am I."

Jack openly despised the idea and constantly argued to his teacher about this transition.

"Brody, I love you. Don't do this man. A new teacher is preposterous! There is nothing that you can't help me achieve that this new 'Indian Chief Wannabe' could."

Needless to say, Jack had no idea what to expect and was honestly a little uncomfortable with the whole idea. He had grown used to his dear friend, Brody and while this didn't end their friendship, he was sure he didn't want a new teacher.

"It is done my friend. You either go with him or you go without."

Jack was devastated. He took it as pure abandonment. In retrospect, Jack thought Brody may have known what he was doing the entire time. A few years later, on a trip to visit Eli at the ranch, Eli had to tell Jack that Brody was found dead in his home. Eli wasn't sure of the details. Jack was devastated and spent days in a lull over the news of his friend's death. Jack still does not know, to this day, how Brody died and he's not sure if he wants to know. It didn't seem that Eli wanted to tell him. Jack just wished his friend was still around.

Jack had taken a friend named Jimbo to the ranch with him on that particular trip. They drove mostly at night to get there and showed up quite late. They were greeted by a few "late-nighters" and shown to their places in the bunkhouse. They were very tired and it didn't take long to fall asleep. The very next day Jack finally met Eli, which was an experience all its own. Jack kept hearing him talk about a "Sweat Lodge". Jack was curious and Brody had said nothing of it until he volunteered Jack to attend. Brody loved to volunteer Jack for different things to test his willingness to experience the world.

"The best way to eliminate self-doubt is to have friends volunteer you for things you don't feel comfortable doing..." Brody would say things like this and then he would giggle. Against what Jack was comfortable with, he agreed to do it.

Jack didn't help with setting up this lodge, and showed up at the last minute, as everyone was preparing to go in. Later he would learn than some take offence to that. Tonight he was a guest and had no idea what he was supposed to do or not do. Eli gave him a few pointers before entering the lodge. He stood tall and proud, shirtless and barefooted, only wearing a pair of sweatpants. He held a turtle shell in his left hand. Jack was sitting and Eli knelt down him, face to face.

"Jack, take off anything metal. It will be hot in here and metal will get hotter than your skin and burn you."

"Oh, alright." replied Jack, unsure that this was a good idea. "Now, if you feel uncomfortable or think you are getting too hot, speak up and you will be honored by everyone here for taking care of yourself."

Jack shook his head in agreement but, thought to himself, *I'm not going to be the sissy of this bunch and tell them I can't hang in as long as them!*

Eli knew, at Jack's young age, he would do that very thing. However, it was important to him that he at least plant the seed and hope that Jack let the tree of "self-care" take root sooner than later. He decided then to watch him carefully and from that moment, Eli made a commitment to Jack that would leave him forever changed. The boy reminded him of himself. His ego was the same ego that Eli had worked on for years before mastering it and being able to make it a tool instead of something debilitating. There were all kinds of people present. Jack looked upon them as he stood outside the strange structure, the sunlight fading into the west. Two of the young men there, only a few years older than Jack, had noticeably long hair, formed in dread locks over the years. They were stripped only to their shorts with bare feet, sitting cross legged in the dirt bearing an expression of peaceful bliss. They didn't speak to him and he thought that was strange.

Jack said to himself, *Here I am going through this whole weird thing and they won't say two words to me.*

The young man with black dread locks began to beat what looked like a homemade drum. Jack observed it closely. It appeared to be a hollowed trunk of some tree that had goat or deer hide drawn tight over its top. The young man warmed the hide by the fire to tighten it and when it seemed tight enough, he sat back and began drumming. The sound echoed through the hills and back around. It was a haunting beat that Jack fell in love with, despite the fact he was uncomfortable here in the first place.

There were a few women there as well. One was an older lady. Despite her age, she still seemed attractive with kind, wise, blue eyes. Her graying hair was pulled back and she wore a long dress that appeared to be a hemp-like material. Another was a very pretty girl who wore a wonderful smile on her face. She had several large tattoos on her upper arms that should have been unattractive to Jack. But, she wore them well and they were tasteful tributes to her life. Honestly, Jack had no clue what they were or what they meant. It appeared that they were words of some ancient descent. He imagined them to say something positive, something profound.

There were children close by. Jack wasn't sure if they would be inside the lodge or not. He truly had no idea what to expect. It turned out they were not. Children were welcome to participate in lodges. However, their parents and the children as well, were also encouraged to wait until they felt that the children were mature enough to remain calm and safe in a small space that held high temperatures at times.

Several others remained outside and inside the little circle of people that would eventually enter this strangely sacred space. The lodge sat directly opposite from a large half-moon berm of broken rock that Jack would learn to be the remnants of hundreds of lodges before that one. Between the two was a large fire to heat the rocks and a small altar of things placed gently in reverence to this whole experience. The people, however different, appeared very kind and it seemed to Jack that no ill will could enter here.

Each member of this group approached Eli and he waived a smoke over them with the feather of a hawk. The smoke was coming from the small turtle shell in his hand that had something burning in it. Jack thought it smelled like sage. They each approached the door of the lodge and turned to each direction, acknowledging it and moving on to the next. Then they bowed down to the Earth and crawled inside the lodge, forming a circle, once inside. Jack was smudged with smoldering sage and told to acknowledge all four directions, which he did, he hoped correctly. Upon entering the lodge, he felt immediately different. It was warm and he felt only positive energy here.

After Eli entered, he pulled the canvas door to the ground behind him and the space was completely dark save the faint glow of the heated red stones located in the center of the space where a shallow hole had been dug to hold them. A language, Jack had yet to understand was spoken in short phrases by a few of the individuals in the lodge, along with some English. It all sounded so beautiful. The air in the lodge was thick like a blanket, protecting all those inside from any harm. The smell of sweet grass and lavender filled their lungs and Jack knew in an instant that he had come home. No one convinced him. He needed no explanation as to why he should love this experience. It was a simple knowing or understanding that this is where he was supposed to be. Eli beat a drum in the lodge and told those present that it represented the ancient heartbeat of our Mother Earth and then the lodge erupted in song.

"The river, she is flowing; flowing and growing! The river she is flowing down to the sea! Mother, carry me! Your child I will always be! Mother, carry me down to the sea!"

Jack was completely blown over by the sound of those voices in that small place. Words could not describe the emotions that came over him and he was moved to tears in an instant. He knew in that moment, nothing beyond where he was mattered. He knew in that moment, everything was going to be alright no matter what. He didn't have to worry about anything in the world because a world of love was created here for him to abide in at that moment in time.

Everyone took turns going around saying something or just passing to the next person. When it came time for Jack to speak, he felt that he made no sense whatsoever. However, he did his best to say how grateful he was to be allowed in this space with the people present. After everyone was done, Eli lifted the door and more rocks were brought in for the second round. Jack looked around and saw people all around him. They were in their own space, completely at peace. Before the door was shut, one of the young men leaned forward toward Jack, over the heat of the rocks. The red glow illuminated his sweaty skin. He looked across the lodge at Jack and said "Welcome Home Brother". He truly felt he was at home; and in that instant made the decision to quit his working life, give up on everything that represented the world of hate and greed that Jack so deeply lamented, and move to the ranch. He knew his young girlfriend wouldn't go. They were on separate paths and Jack saw those paths only growing farther apart. There was just a solid knowledge that this is what he was going to do. This is where he belonged.

After the second door, Jack had to step out for a moment to get some air. As he stood there, his head began to spin and he passed out and woke up moments later. Jack never told anyone that this happened and he knew he should have. He was just so wrapped up in the moment that he felt he couldn't stay out of the lodge. He felt a strong desire to finish it and also felt strongly that this new Great Spirit would guide him safely through. The last two doors were more intense that the first two and they all lay there with every door open after it was over just letting the cool night air sweep over their sweat soaked bodies. Jack was among family now. They accepted him and allowed him the honor of participating in this sacred tradition. He was also ravenously hungry, and after a while, they made their way back to the house and feasted on chips and salsa, cheese and crackers, and fruits. Jack slept better that night than he had in years.

Jack woke up the next morning with the kind of conviction that you can only get with a true spiritual experience of that magnitude. He felt amazing, unstoppable and truly energized beyond what he had ever been before. He called his girlfriend and the feeling was not mutual. He knew it wouldn't be. This was a very difficult thing for him even to this day. He wanted to explain his experience of the lodge. He wanted others to embrace it as he did. He wanted them to have that enlightenment, to experience that kind of closeness with other human beings, and to see our Earth as a life giving mother. But this is something sacred and for it to be forced on anyone only devalues the lodge and creates an unsafe place for everyone. It gives the experience a price and a tangible value and nothing of the sort should ever be forced. It should be sought after. Jack knew this and let the lodge remain an introverted experience that he only shared if someone sought it out through him.

To Jack, the lodge is a place to honor our ancestors and to thank them for their examples and lessons. It is a place to honor our Creator and ourselves. We can pray for one another. We can share our feelings openly and unashamedly. Anyone who understands the lodge could, in fact, get a lot out of participating in one, regardless of personal religious creed. It embodies the things that are universal and omnipresent in western and eastern religions. We treat one another with love. Each person's presence is acknowledged and appreciated. Jack thought of the lodge as his church. He didn't wish to be in a building with one hundred other people worshiping something they cannot grasp or conceive. He wanted to dig his toes into the mud and sing a song that honored the fruits of his labor, the blessings which he had received, and the spirit of love that is present in all of us. He didn't want to hope and pray that a god would give him a better life. He wanted to create a better life.

Jack thought it ridiculous to want to blame a tempting demon for his own personal screw-ups. He wanted to own them and change himself into a better person. The lodge creates a space that people can hold one another accountable to their own desires. It is a space where they can encourage one another and share their struggles instead of hoarding them as secrets.

CHAPTER EIGHT

Jack continued past the medicine wheel and the lodge, making his way toward Eli's tree house. The road under his feet was no longer packed hard from regular traffic. It had grown over and was filled with standing water in places where tires used to travel. The little scrub oaks to his right tried hard to emulate their brothers to the north, giving little rattles as the wind continued to blow its breath across the land. The birds did not sing and he had not seen an animal, not so much as a gray squirrel, since he had been here. The last hint of any noticeable life was the robin and the hoot owl this morning. It was as if the world had died with the awakening of the sun.

As Jack approached the tree house, he was appalled at its appearance. The windows were all broken and the door stood open wide. The porch outside was piled with trash and tools, end cuts of lumber and clothing. The stairway had fallen apart and had been replaced by a rusty bent ladder. Jack looked away from the tree house and peered forward down the path toward the new lodge that was still about ten years old. The path grew smaller and the trees hung over the tiny path. Jack thought he saw movement in the trees. *Could it be a deer?* He crouched and inched his way closer to the little rattling scrub oaks to stay out of sight. The wind blew out of the north and Jack tried to stay directly parallel to the animal so as to keep it from smelling him and running away. Jack wanted terribly to see it. He somehow knew it would help make sense of some of this. If he could just see a deer, a hog or a turkey, he would at least know that this wasn't some supernatural experience in which he was stuck. The movement continued ever so slightly at the base of the trees. It was dark in color. Just as it moved out into the road, Jack's hopes were dashed and his heart filled with fear. It was the black spot. It appeared as a shadow on the ground. The dark splotch upon the earth grew and shrunk. But it remained as black as the night, resting along the path. Jack stood to get a better look. The shadow turned as if it saw him standing there and immediately dashed across the path and into the trees, breaking twigs and pushing leaves aside as it retreated.

Jack stood as still as he could, his heart pounding ferociously. *What was that thing?* He screamed in his mind. Jack wanted to turn and run. But he could not move his legs for the paralyzing fear. This time the fear would not leave and it settled in his bones like a crippling disease. Jack felt old and decrepit. He was sick to his stomach and fell back to the ground throwing up the coffee Janice had made him earlier. His eyes watered as he coughed and dry heaved.

Jack wiped his face against his flannel sleeve, still on his knees and bent over. He looked up toward the path and back at the tree house. He slowly stood using all of his strength to get up. The tree house, although only twenty feet away, might has well have been a mile. *Where has my strength gone?* His arms and legs felt as if they were weighted down. Jack pushed through the weights as hard as he could and began the trek to the rusty ladder.

By the time he made it to the ladder, Jack was breathing heavily and exhausted. He flung his right arm upon one of the rusty rungs, then the other, and hung his head in despair. Jack stood there panting for a bit and finally started to climb. Every rung was coarse and painful and left a dark line of blood red rust across his palms. Jack reached the top and pulled himself up on the porch. He rolled to his back and took a rest; his heart was pounding, and he was breathing as hard as he could. He lay there for all of ten minutes, trying to rest as much as possible before standing. He rolled back to his stomach and pushed himself upward to a standing position, careful not to fall off the porch to the ground, fifteen feet below.

Once he was standing, he felt a bit better and made his way through the open door into the dark tree house. Jack lit an oil lamp that was sitting on a small TV tray that Eli had used for a desk. As the oil lamp's flame lit the room, Jack could see paper all over the floor; piles of it strewn like it was at the bunkhouse. But there was considerably more here. The one room house smelled of mildew from the broken windows letting in the rain.

Jack saw a book on the couch and walked over to it. He bent down and picked it up, turned around and fell back on the couch.

"Eli must've been reading this. He usually puts a book up forever once he's read it." Jack said aloud.

Eli often wrote notes in his books and Jack thought maybe there would be some clue that Eli had left behind, anything that could make Jack able to save this place. Jack wanted dearly to be the Hero he knew he was. It was just a matter of finding the right information and then he could save the ranch.

He looked at the cover to see the title and noticed the top layer had been scraped off where the title would usually lay. He opened the cover to look for a title page and further noticed that it had been torn out. *How strange?* Thought Jack. He flipped a few pages and something caught his eye. Looking down onto the page, someone had scrawled in big black letters, "I ALREADY KNOW!!!!" The de'ja'vu set in heavy. Jack had been here before. It was his writing in the book, not Eli's.

Jack slammed the book shut and threw it across the room as hard as he could. He screamed as it smashed a little more glass out of an already broken window. As the sun began to set in the west, the Shadow crept freely at the base of the tree house, completely undetected. As the waning light retreated with the sun, the Shadow began its journey up the eastern side of the large poles that held the tree house in the air. It crept into the house through the broken glass and snuffed the oil lamp out with a cold gust.

Jack was alone again. He curled himself onto to the couch and prayed for the sun, just as he had many nights before. It was another cycle of misery. It was another night of rolling all over the floor in a panic, trying to evade his Shadow that would certainly end his existence and the existence of everything that was left here, this place he called home. It crept all over the room, rustling the papers Jack had laid all about the floor in order to hear the beast that was Jack's Shadow.

He could hear Eli and Janice pleading and crying at the bottom. "Jack, please read it. Please Jack, you already know! Please!" He tried to shut them out. He tried with all his might to ignore their pleas. "Jack, we'll do it together! We're not leaving you Jack, even if it kills us both!"

Jack began his wailing until they would shut up and leave him alone. This was a battle he could not win. The Shadow might as well have him. He could never beat it and it was futile to stay up all night and try. But the fear of it grabbing a hold was more than he could bear. Jack wrestled with it all the night through, screaming out and jumping from one end of the room to the other in a worthless attempt to evade the Shadow.

CHAPTER NINE

Hero pushed through the vines along-side the river and stayed crouched low to the sandy earth. He could hear Jack close behind, wailing and screaming. His voice was dark and he heaved and growled in between screams as he began to close in.

"C'mon, you bastard! Come out here! I want to see you run! I want to watch you bleed, you piece of trash!"

Tears came to Hero's eyes. *What had happened to him?*

Jack was taken over now by the Shadow. The Shadow had complete control and Hero was but a faded dream that Jack could only hate. Jack was full of fear. He was full of despair and his only answer to the despair was rage. Rage filled his body and seeped from the pores of his flesh, boiling to the surface and pouring out upon the earth and everything he came into contact with.

The animals had all left. The wind was the only sound. The river was dark. Black water covered from view by a dense fog, crept up the bank and rested at the base of the tall, limestone bluffs. The bluffs reached high in the sky, three hundred feet or so. The caves no longer appeared to be little safe havens, opening their mouths to passers-by. Now, they were open as if they belonged on the face of an old man, desperately screaming lonely cries of the great river it once looked over and fed. Eli and Janice lay wasted in the shell of their once amazing land. They could do nothing but sit and watch it all die. They had tried desperately to save him. But even on the good days, woke in the mornings confused, living it all over again until the Shadow returned to consume him. Sometimes it would take hours and sometimes, when Jack was progressing it would take days to rear its ugly head and consume Jack once again.

This was as bad as it had ever been. Since it took its first hold, Jack had never fully come out of its grasp on his mind. He would spend a day to a few days confused about why Eli and Janice were so forlorn and why the ranch was so gloomy. He would argue with Eli as to why the ranch was suffering in its appearance. Eli and Janice had tried some time to explain what was going on with him but, it was to no avail. He listened to Eli's "Shadow Story" and pretended to take it to heart, all the while simply seeing it as some of Eli's "Hocus Pocus". It was all very metaphorical to Jack and he never really took it to heart. He could simply see the points as great parables to live by.

Of course they were great Ideas, with wonderful storylines and characters. Hell, I could write that down and make millions. Eli almost believes it himself! Jack would tell himself this and never, for one instance, did he think it could be real. Yet, here it happened. Jack's Shadow was anchored firmly within him and it was alive. It was him. Yet it acted separate and apart from who Jack really wanted to be.

It was so bad that Eli told Janice he thought this was the last time they would see Jack. "Janice, Hero will have to kill him." he had told her.

Janice argued that suggestion and begged Eli to think of something else. "You know him. Eli! You can break through the Shadow!"

But he could not. It was something stronger than Eli's will. That didn't even come into play. It was a matter of fact. Jack chose somewhere along the way. Somehow, he chose the Shadow. Once he did, the Shadow came back and Jack had come to the point now, that he could not control it alone. The Shadow came to him when it wanted and no matter how hard Jack ran to hide, the Shadow continuously consumed him.

Hero was all that stood between Jack's total destruction and the destruction of everything in his life's experience. But, Hero was on the run to save his own existence. For without him, the only hope was that Jack's neutral self could muster any of Hero's traits. That was next to impossible. The more likely scenario was Jack being left alone to this land and terrorizing it and everything that it came in contact with for the rest of his soul's existence.

Throughout the infinite Universe, Jack would be forever doomed to recreate this with each life given him by the Great Being. Every chance would be re-lived without a Hero and another must be built if he was to succumb to Jack's Shadow. But, that was unheard of. It was unfathomable in the laws of the Universe, if the Universe had any law at all.

Jack felt consumed and sick. He was a under the complete control of the Shadow and he could not let it go. There were so many things wrong. There were so many things to hate. Everything was hatred. Everything was red with rage. Jack's only comfort was to pillage, to destroy, and to kill the life in everything he saw. At first, it scared him, the power of destruction. But he allowed himself to finally succumb; and after a while, it began to feel good. Later, it began to be something he needed. Now, it was all that he was, save the faint memory of something sweet. Jack saw that nowhere, now. He remembered that it had once existed. Something sweet had existed somewhere in the trees, somewhere in the bluffs. Somewhere from within the earth, something warm exuded outward and touched the souls of man.

Jack could think no more of it and fell to his knees heaving up something from his stomach that he had no memory of consuming. It was warm, black and angry. Jack feared it had come from the Hero. *The Hero is poisoning me. He is killing me a little more each instant. I have to grow. I have to consume. Where is he? The Hero must die! Everything will die until I reach him and kill him by my hand.*

Jack's thoughts raced. His head spun with fear and confusion. He had not yet mastered this new, exciting possession. This power was immensely sickening almost as much as it was enthralling. His power succeeded life. It destroyed everything that threatened his purpose. His body tingled with the itch to move with hasty hatred, with power and force over all things. He was the omnipotent, and it felt good to be God.

The flow of the river had slowed. The water was only stagnant ooze and sucker fish lined the rocky bank, their stench wafting through the chilly fall wind that continued to make those oak leaves quiver. Hero kept a distance from Jack that was safe enough to remain unharmed, all the while remembering that it was his duty to stay within distance to strike if needed. His knife unsheathed, Hero cut a thin, un-flexible branch from a sapling and began to sharpen one end to a point. He whittled and prayed under his breath, uttering hopeful thoughts for Jack to listen to him, once captured. Hero knew this battle would be one of the hardest he had ever fought for Jack. This time, he was fighting Jack in the flesh and although Jack rarely ever realized it, they were usually battling side-by-side instead of against one another.

Once the point was made on the sapling, Hero began to dig in the sand as vigorously as possible without making noise. He dug about twelve to thirteen inches down, cut the sapling off at about six inches and rammed the stick, point upwards, as hard as he could down into the earth. The pointed sapling stuck upward inside. Hero hurriedly filled the hole with loose sand and drying Sycamore leaves. He spread the remaining leaves all about the ground to camouflage his ground trap. He didn't want to kill Jack. Although he knew it to be a possibility, Hero couldn't dream of such a fate for Jack. There was so much more the young man could do. There was so much more potential energy left in his young mind that Hero was obligated still, at this point in Jack's present life, to show him his potential, to eradicate the darkness, to fight side-by-side, to save Jack from his very own Shadow.

Hero stood over his trap and thought to himself, *This may not work at all. This may be terrible. But it is what must be done.* Hero worried that the recovery process of a stick through the foot may allow the Shadow to creep directly back inside of him. Even if he had a great break-through and was able to help Jack understand what was happening to him, Hero knew the fact that Jack would have to lay down and heal his physical body would provide idle time. Hero understood that some philosophies from the Christian faith and many other faiths were very applicable if not nearly synonymous to the Universal Laws. "Idle time" really was the "Devil's" invitation. It would take a lot of work to keep Jack alive and within Hero's grasp. Hero was not at all in the business of doubting. However, he was a realistic entity and Hero knew that this may require help.

The wind began to pick up a bit and Hero knew that Jack was beginning to get closer. He could smell the Shadow and the darkness crept over the ground. Jack's breathing was labored and contained an intense rattle from deep within his body. Hero listened to it carefully and hoped Jack's strength hadn't grown too far for his trap not to work. He could hear Jack's steps. They were still labored and his toes drug the sand behind him. The Shadow was still in its infancy as a host, and was still holding Jack up on its own. But his strength would soon grow to the point that Jack's full range of motion would return and his strength would grow to that which was Hero's. Hero knew he could not let that happen.

As Jack began to close in, Hero pulled some of his hair from his head and placed it around the ground trap in a circle. He ducked low and darted off into the brush, away from the river at the base of the bluffs. Crouched in a sort of football stance, not moving even an inch with his pack secured to his back and the large hunting knife strapped securely to his leg, Hero waited in the brush. His long hair shifted and blew over his eyes with the increasing wind. He dared not try to brush it away. He held his eyes open and over the ground trap as intently as possible. Any movement would possibly alert Jack away from the trap and toward Hero. The fate for Jack would be death; and although Jack didn't have all of his strength yet, the Shadow had all of its senses.

The wind was now blowing at a terrible speed. The trees creaked eerily overhead, screaming out to Hero. They begged him to stop. They pleaded for their lives to him. Hero had to ignore their pleas for the greater good in the current situation. It pulled at him and broke his heart to hear the collective cries of the Earth around him. But, he knew he must remain still and focused. Jack stepped up the bank from the river, only his head appearing first. He walked jagged and stiff. His flannel shirt was torn at the sleeves and the chest. Only a few buttons held the midriff together. His shirt fell ragged upon his sand caked blue jeans. They were no longer blue. Now they were the color of the sand that Jack had fallen into multiple times while trying to walk. His jeans were wet with the black stagnant river water halfway up his shins and Jack's shoes were untied and barely on his feet. Hero listened intently as Jack drug his toes behind him with each grueling step. It was as if something was holding him upright, and Hero knew that was absolutely true.

Hero's attention rose to Jack's face and he fought back hard, the tears that wanted so badly to flow. Jack's face was contorted in a terrible twist that read sheer terror. His eyes were dark yellow around the iris, which had all filled to black. His boyish face was twisted into that of a terrified old man that is about to die, but has so much left to say. His hair, always in a traveling youngster's style of happily disheveled was now matted and covered in sand and soil. His breathing continued to rattle deep in his chest and he moaned cries with every single step. "I smell you! I'm gonna find you, you son of a bitch!" Jack sneered up at the trees.

As he approached the ground trap, Jack stopped in his tracks and looked straight forward. His filthy nose twitched like a dog's when it smells an animal to chase. Jack's head spun sharp directly to Hero's position in the brush. Hero knew that he had been seen and closed his eyes only for a moment to regain focus and prepare to fight. In that moment, Hero committed to killing Jack. If he had in fact seen him, the Shadow would not stop until Jack or Hero lay dead on the sandy ground. He had the upper hand and although the Shadow knew that, it was consumed with hate and would fight like a scared animal. It would kill itself before it ever gave in.

Hero's eyes flashed open and light poured out from them onto the leaves of the scrub oak. But the light pierced the dense fog no further. Hero stared directly into Jack's eyes waiting for them to indicate any sudden movement forward. Neither of them moved a muscle for what seemed like an eternity to Hero. Suddenly, Jack, with his eyes still fixed in the same direction, seemingly upon Hero's position, began to slowly kneel down. He was standing very closely to the ground trap. As Hero had hoped, Jack knelt all the way to the ground and picked up some of the loose hair Hero had laid down. He held it between three of his fingers and twisted it back and forth, forming a ball and let it roll back into his palm. Jack then lowered his nose to the hair and sniffed at it closely. He reeled backward in disgust and dropped the hair, laying on his side and dry heaving in the sand and Sycamore leaves. As Jack twisted himself back to a crouched position, Hero used the noisy opportunity to shift his weight only a little. Jack slowly rose a little, not yet to a full standing position, and took a step forward. *Yes, Jack. Keep moving, brother.* Hero thought to himself. Jack did. He took one more step and his left foot went deep into the hole. Jack fell to the ground again, this time with a roar of pain and fear. The sharp sapling split his foot open at the sole and extruded from the top, pushing bone upward and squirting blood that quickly filled his shoe. The snap of the bones could be easily heard from Hero's position at the time that Jack fell. Now, nothing could be heard all across the watery valley except Jack's terrified screams and rage-filled roars.

Jack twisted and scooted his body as hard as he could backward, trying to pull his foot off of the stick. But his strength was shallow and he could not budge it. Hero knew it was time to confront him. He stood from the brush and walked slowly toward his beloved Jack.

Jack, my brother, I am you and you are me. Let me help, please. Hero said calmly.

"Get away from me! Get away!" Jack roared back.

Jack, I beg you to let me help. I...

"I said get away! I'll kill you where you stand!"

Jack pulled the gun from his jeans and pointed it directly at Hero. He pulled the trigger quickly without aiming and shot into the trees behind him. Hero hit the ground hard and rolled to the side. Jack took time to aim. He pulled the trigger again. This time, nothing happened. There was not even a click. The trigger just depressed with no tension. The firing pin obviously never struck the primer. Jack looked at the gun. It had jammed. The one spent shell lay vertical in the chamber and was being crushed under the compression of the slide. The firing mechanism was covered in sand and dirt. It was useless, now. He jerked hard against the stick and still could not pull his body off of it. Jack threw the gun hard toward the brush as far as he could and Hero stood up. He was fury embodied and pounced on Jack, pinning his arms back to the earth.

Jack's head writhed back and forth, rising up occasionally and snapping his teeth at Hero, growling like an animal trapped. Hero glared at him and waited for him to tire. After a few seconds of struggling against Hero, Jack began to lose strength and fell limp, breathing as hard as he ever had. Hero raised his own head back and brought his forehead down hard, with a crashing blow to Jack's nose. Blood poured from his nostrils, over his cheeks and back into his eyes. Jack could not breathe. Now he could not see. The fight was won. Hero did not have to kill him. He rose up away from Jack laying on the ground and smiled proudly. There was hope. There was hope to make it out of here with Jack in one piece and the Shadow, never gone, but at least held at bay.

Hero learned an important lesson on this day. The Shadow will always be present. If fed, it will grow in strength and power. If Jack fed Hero, the opposite would occur. So, in essence, it was up to Jack how this played out. But, Hero still had power and was able to create an opportunity for Jack to make a choice. But Jack was enveloped with rage. The Shadow had a hold of him like never before. The battle was only beginning and Jack had many stages to overcome, the first being his misconception that that Hero was taking liberty from him rather than granting him the power to be the greatest version of himself that he could ever be.

Chapter Ten

Hero laid Jack in a large cave that rested about one hundred and fifty feet directly up the bluff. The cave had a large enough mouth that it would be simple for Hero to walk around upright and work with Jack once he began to feel better. Here, he would be safe from most animals and would be given the opportunity to heal his torn foot. A clean, fresh water spring poured from deep within the cave. The water was pure enough that Hero could give it to Jack without fear of him getting sick. Hero had previously set up an old army cot in the cave and laid wool blankets on it. Now, Jack lay under them sleeping. He did not sleep well, however. He was restless, sick and still emitted and occasional shriek of desperation. His screams un-nerved Hero. But, he understood, this was the process. The Shadow was still very much present. It lay dormant waiting for Hero to let his guard down.

Hero worked diligently to not let that happen. He poured his attention into Jack. He stayed awake while Jack screamed, never letting his eyes close, except for a moment here and there when Jack had calmed down. He forced Jack to drink the water even if he didn't want to and continued to change the dressing on his left foot. Jack never once appeared grateful. He remained angry and stood steadfast against his treatment. He cursed Hero with every breath. Jack tried terribly hard to make Hero angry, to make him leave, to get him to do anything but help. It was no use though. Hero stayed with him through the name calling, the cursing and the abuse. Hero loved Jack and understood they were one another. Jack had yet to understand this and continued to see Hero as the enemy.

As much as Hero despised to tie Jack up, he had to when leaving the cave. Jack was healing very slowly as the Shadow still tugged at his true potential. He needed medicine and Hero knew exactly what to get. But it meant leaving Jack alone. It was a risk that must be taken, however. Jack screamed loudly as Hero tightened the cord around his arms and torso. Jack cried for him to stop, that Hero was hurting him. But Hero knew that it was just a ploy from the Shadow to gain strength, to fight again, this time to the death. It was difficult for Hero. But it had to be done and this was the only way. It wasn't easy. But nothing worth fighting for ever was. Hero saw Jack's potential. He knew Jack could be a great force of destruction just as he could be a warrior of peace, a defender of innocence. Hero would give his life to save Jack. He knew this to be a possible outcome. But he held steadfast to his mission; *Save Jack!   Teach Jack to be the new Hero!*

After Jack was tied up securely, Hero left the cave and climbed down to the river and found a break in the bluffs to walk upward on a hillside. This was his best chance at good roots and animals that would not be poisonous. It had been two days since either of them had eaten anything. Hero's hunger was insatiable and was beginning to cloud his judgment. He knew it was time for both of them to eat. Jack's backpack had been left in Eli's tree house and Hero dared not leave him long enough to go back for it. That would take at least two hours, at a running pace and Jack was not ready to be left alone that long. Hero had a keen eye for Ginseng that was left over from the spring and summer. It was a wonderful energy supplement. He filtered through hillside plants until he found enough of the root to last a little while. He went on to pick the Yellow Dock Root out of the hills as well. It would be good for Jack's healing foot. It would help his digestion and over-all health, if made into a tea. Hero prayed to find a few left over Sweet Gum leaves to place directly on Jack's injured foot. But there were none to be found. The Sweet Gums had all gone away between the harsh fall and the Shadow's presence. The animals stayed at bay as well. Any animals Hero could find were animals that lived in the ground which typically meant insects. They weren't the most appetizing treat. But, it would have to suffice for now.

Back at the cave, Jack lay still in the darkness, breathing slowly as if asleep. But he was anything but asleep. The Shadow was very much alive inside him. It argued to break the cords.

Break them you weakling! Break them! Set me free, Jack! I am all you have now, boy! You are just a boy without me, Jack! Do you want power? No! You want to be his slave, don't you?

The Shadow laughed at him and jeered at his weakness. Jack could not see it as anything but his own weakness and pled to the Shadow for help.

"I cannot do it alone! I need you, Shadow! Please! I cannot break the cord myself! I don't want to be his slave! I will never be!"

Jack pulled hard against the cord. He jerked his body around as much as he could. But the cord was too strong. Eventually, due to his constant jerking and twisting the cot tipped over to its right side. Jack immediately felt the blood rush to his injured foot and wailed loudly, loud enough for Hero to hear. Jack lay there and cried. The watery cave trickled incessantly and the darkness permeated every corner. Jack felt the cold stone floor heavy on his right shoulder and his injured foot now bled again out onto the ground. He lay there helpless.

Hero heard the wail and immediately began making his way back to the cave. Instead of going down to the river, he saved five minutes or so by gliding directly across the hillside and scaling the bluff to get to Jack. Hero knew Jack was too weak to escape. But, he feared that if somehow he was able to free himself of the cord, he would only kill himself trying to scale the bluff or navigate the cave. Hero moved across the bluff like he had been born to do this all along. His fingers grasped the limestone rock crevices with amazing strength and his feet propelled him like a monkey in the trees. Hero was agile in the forest and it showed with his great ability to move when he needed.

As what was left of the sun began to fade behind the opposing bluffs, from the other side of the river, Jack swung around the mouth of the cave and landed inside the dark crevice. He could see very little. But, it was obvious that Jack had fallen over and was struggling and crying in an effort to free himself.

Jack, my brother, stop this foolishness. Can't you see that I am here to help?

"Just let me die here, Hero!" Jack exclaimed between heaving coughs from deep within his chest.

You're going to get your chance Jack, if you keep up this nonsense.

Hero tilted the cot back upward and loosened the cords around Jack, just enough to get one arm out. Hero massaged Jack's arm and then the other, careful to keep one tied down. Hero worked on his legs and the one foot that was not in excruciating pain. Hero washed the injured foot with the cold spring water. The fresh blood flowed around his ankle and over the heel, following the stream of cold spring water. It splashed pink on the ground and pooled around the base of the cot. Jack relaxed a little bit and began to appear asleep again. While his breathing calmed, Hero stepped to the mouth of the cave and gathered a little firewood. He brought it back in and started a small fire to heat the big room, just a little. He knew not to overheat the cave as the expanding rock may break loose and come crashing down. Hero boiled some of the spring water and Yellow Dock Root down to a tea. He put some of the beetles and leftover worms in the boil at the last minute, so as to not cook away too much of the good vitamins and minerals that Jack needed.

When it was done, Hero woke Jack, loosened the cords enough for Jack to sit up, and then immediately tied his hands back down. This left Jack in a seated position. With his hands tied, there was nothing he could do except head-butt and bite. Jack was too tired to do either and although Hero's concoction was disgusting, he was starving and weak and he drank every bit of it. It filled his belly and immediately Jack remembered again, that something sweet. There it was on the outskirts of his memory. What was this sweet thing?

It's nothing you want, Jack! It's what got you here. It's what made you weak, Jack! They sell you sweet and you only get the bitter, boy!

Jack closed his eyes. He wanted to shut the Shadow out. But he could not. It was too loud. Even in moments of clarity, which were still cloudy and ever rare, the Shadow constantly spoke to him. It told him he could not. It told him he was too weak. It told him to destroy anything that said different. Jack obeyed because there were no other options he could see. As far as he was concerned, he was too weak. He was full of fear and could never defeat Hero, unless he could trick him.

Once Jack's moaning subsided, Hero stepped out of the mouth of the cave and crouched low on a rocky ledge, over-looking the dark expanse of river that had faded into the coming night. The wind continued to rattle the oak leaves and Hero felt something cold land upon his arm. He looked down. It was a snowflake. It was the first snow of a long winter that Jack and Hero would sit in this cave and heal. Jack would try many times to escape. Hero would remain faithful to him and pull him back in to safety time and time again.

Eli and Janice would sit, forlorn. They waited while Hero tried to save Jack and bring him back from the river to save their land. They held to one another for strength. They argued that Hero could never succeed and that Jack was too far gone. But it was worth the chance. They had nothing to lose but their lives. The land had already been swallowed and consumed by the Shadow's fear. It would take a Hero to save it. It would be a collective effort.

CHAPTER ELEVEN

For five long months, Hero stayed with Jack in the cave. For the first three, he remained tied to the cot and Hero only slowly extended his trust after that. The winter was long and cruel with hateful winds direct from the north. They blew into the mouth of the cave and Hero had long since moved their camp deeper inside to escape its harsh bite. That, however almost completely obliterated the comfort of a fire. The only days a fire's warmth could be enjoyed were when the north winds calmed enough to move back out to the mouth of the cave for short intervals. The cave's constant temperature protected them from the winter's bitter cold and the fresh spring water kept their thirst quenched. Obtaining food was a difficult ordeal. In order to hunt, Hero had to travel far enough away to where animals remained. This meant Jack had to be secured for long periods of time until Hero returned. By the time he got back, Jack was often so angry that trust had to be re-built again and again. The longer they stayed, the better Jack got and the closer the animals came.

Hero had even started to hear a few squirrels overhead in the mornings, chirping their songs to one another, alerting one another of human or predator presence. The river had begun to flow. The water was less stagnant and cloudy. Occasionally, Hero was able to snatch a Small Mouth Bass from under a rock to add to their depleted diet. Jack had greater moments of clarity. He still was very unsure of what the sweet memory could be and he still resented it for the most part. But, there existed in him a desire to learn a little more each day about who Hero was and what his role was with Jack.

The nights were the most difficult. The Shadow was more apt to return when loneliness prevailed. For Jack, that seemed to be in the evening. The Shadow told Jack time and time again that he needed something outside of him to make all of this make sense.

You aren't enough, Jack, it would squeal. Before long, Jack would toss and turn at the thought of his own insufficient self. Whatever the Shadow said was law and Jack had to be thoroughly convinced of anything that Hero had taught him over and over. Usually, it only stuck for a day or so. They were making some manner of progress.

Hero wondered, What is it going to take to build him up and forget the Shadow? Jack couldn't seem to shake it completely. The Shadow remained steadfast and strong. There were only moments it proudly showed its face through Jack. But, it was always there in his doubt and sinister outlook. There was never a smile. Nothing seemed to ever be enough. Jack was always worried about starving to death even though Hero had fed him even when things were not plentiful. Now that the spring was in full effect, Jack complained about the bugs they had so earnestly begged for in the winter. Now, they were only a nuisance.

"Hero, when can I go back up the bluff to Eli and Janice?"

You're not ready yet, Jack. But we are making progress, my brother.

"Why do you call me that, Hero?"

I told you that we are the same people, you and me.

"That doesn't make any sense, Hero."

That's why I just call you my brother.

Jack rolled his eyes in annoyance. The cave had become claustrophobic to him. *Here I sit in the dark. The bluest sky ever is just beyond my reach! I want to leave! I want to explore! I want to go back to the Main House and sit with my friends!* He wanted to sit in the Main House and eat Eli's famous Buckwheat pancakes and drink Janice's coffee. Or better yet a glass of her homemade wine! *This cave living is for the birds, or the bats to be more precise.* Jack rationalized his reason for needing to leave with every single innocent pleasure he had enjoyed during a happier, healthier life that he loved so dearly, still. But his ego still could not let him differentiate what was false or true in his life.

Hero had stopped tying him up a few months ago and Jack was able to sit on his own and wait for him to return. The Shadow spoke to him sometimes. But for the most part, Jack was able to tune it out until Hero returned, until today. He was fed up with being closed off from the world and just simply wanted to walk outside. *What would be the harm? Just a simple walk... Enjoy nature... Isn't that what he wants me to do anyway?*

Hero looked down at him. *I'm going to go find some food. Are you alright to sit here for a little while until I get back?*

"Yes, of course." Jack said, obviously irritated at the question.

I mean it, Jack. Right here is where you will be. Do not put me in the position to tie you down again.
"Stop worrying! Isn't that what you tell me to do?"

Hero smiled and pulled his hunting knife tight against his leg. His hair hung down in his face. Both of them were filthy. Neither of them had had more than a spring water scrub-down in over five months. Hero's face was darkened by the soot of the fires he tended and his body was scarred by the countless days and nights of scaling the icy bluffs and hunting for food to keep them both alive. Jack was ashen from lack of sunlight and severe malnutrition. Dark circles enveloped his eyes. But, Hero could not let him build too much strength until he was ready. Otherwise there would be another battle and Hero may have to kill Jack if the Shadow gained enough strength to fight again. Hero jerked his pack up off the ground and slung it over his tattered right shoulder.

I'll be back in less than an hour. Why don't you read the books I left? They're over in that corner by the cot.

"I may just do that."

Hero darted out of the cave and set out to hunt their supper. Jack had no intention of staying in the cave and intended to simply wait for the coast to be clear. But out of pure fear, he sat waiting well beyond that moment. Hero's power was strong and Jack was weak. Jack felt strongly that Hero would know any move he made. So, he waited, not only for the "clear coast"; he also waited for his own nerves to calm down before he made any move whatsoever.

Inch by inch, Jack scooted to the mouth of the enormous cave. Soon, he felt the breeze across his bare feet and the sun broke through to warm his knees. Jack continued to scoot until his feet were dangling from the mouth and he looked down at the river valley. He was immediately consumed with excitement. There it lay beneath him. The vast river valley was his to explore. It belonged to him and he felt he had dominion over it. Something screamed for him to climb down and run to it. He wondered, *Is this the Shadow? No way! There's no way the Shadow would tell me to do something so wonderful! The Shadow would tell me to fear it, right?*

Jack clearly remembered Hero's instruction to not leave. But he thought, *Hero cannot be right all of the time! I am going! I'll show him I can do it! He'll have more faith in me when he sees that I came right back after having a good run along the river!*

Out of the cave, Jack climbed. The warm spring air touched his pale skin and Jack was invigorated with energy. He shouldn't have this much get up and go. But he did, nonetheless. He scaled the bluff, however awkwardly, right down to the river. Carefully, he placed each foot in the correct crevice and lowered himself to the bottom. As his feet touched the sandy earth, the memory of his power over this place returned. He remembered how he controlled it. Jack jumped upward and slammed his feet against the earth. His wound had healed well over the winter and he only felt a slight tingle from the impact. *The gun…. Where was the gun?* Jack looked intently for the place that he and Hero had fought.

He knew it to be close by this spot. Hero did not pull him far from the fight to the cave. The trip was mostly an upward one. Jack's eyes spanned the river bank, looking for any depression. *Ha! That was five months ago! There won't be any remnants on the ground of that fight!* Jack began to pace back and forth, up and down the river bank, stomping his feet in frustration. He wore a grimaced face and became more and more filled with energy. *This doesn't make sense. I should be tired. Maybe this exactly what I need. I need to get out and move!*

Jack stamped around and finally stubbed is big toe on a stick that shot straight up from the sand. He back away and observed it. "Well, you're in a strange spot" he said aloud. The stick was a walnut sapling that had four ribbons tied to the top; one red, one yellow, one white and the other black. Jack stepped back further and the memory came back to him. *This was the spot. There it was*

---

by the bank of the river, just down from the scrub brush from which Hero had jumped. Jack knelt by it and remembered the battle. He remembered how Hero had tricked him and split his foot in two with the sapling. Hero had held him down and would not let him get up. He took Jack's power away from him. Jack wondered why. *Who gives me the power to take and to give? He could not have just talked me down, if I was out of control? What was the need for hurting me and putting me through the misery of the cave for an entire winter? Where is the gun?* Jack allowed the Shadow's doubts to consume him. He looked back toward the bluffs where he had thrown the .380 pistol and walked toward the area.

It did not take too terribly long after searching under the prickly brush to see it shining there in the dark sand. It was awfully corroded and looked barely useable, if useable at all. Jack reached down and picked it up. The slide was still halfway back with a spent cartridge sticking a little bit out of the chamber. Jack turned the gun upside down and pulled the slide back a little further. It was hard to pull back. Yet, with a little effort, it finally broke free. Jack's eyes closed and he fell into the void that lived in his mind. The spent casing fell to the earth and Jack, in one swift motion, turned the gun right side up and jerked back hard on the slide again, letting it fall into place. The sound was enthralling. Jack could hear the next shell fall into place in the chamber and he held the pistol outward wearing an evil look on his face. His eyes opened and they shone again. His feet dug into the sand and Jack listened intently to the Shadow as it spoke clearly to him.

This is your power, Jack. This is all you need to come back to me.

The Shadow spoke loud and clear and Jack listened. The Shadow had never hurt him or held him down. The Shadow just wanted Jack to be happy and powerful. Jack had omnipotence with the Shadow and it felt much better than being under Hero's oppressive thumb all of the time. He resented Hero. But, he knew he could not fight him off right now. That would take some time and patience. For all that Hero knew, as of now, Jack was sitting and waiting patiently for him to return.

"Shit! What time is it?" Jack said aloud. He knew he had no way of telling real time out here. But by his best guess, Hero would be back any minute. Jack lowered the gun and stuck it in the waist of his pants. He climbed back up the bluff as far as he could without taking a breath and turned around to look for Hero. Jack could hear him coming back, his footsteps at a fast running pace, though he could not see him yet.

****

Hero had gathered one squirrel in a trap he had set two days prior and had filled his small leather pouch with beetles and grub worms. He wanted to take Jack back, as much as Jack wanted to be back, to Eli and Janice's home. But it was just too early. Jack had made definite progress. However, the Shadow continued to knock on the door of Jack's mind at every available opportunity. It was a fine balance to keep Jack in check and to keep him from resenting Hero to the point where he left. Hero just did the best that he could. He hated to leave him. But there was no other way to get food. Although the animals were beginning to come back, they were very aware of Jack's presence and would leave as soon as he got within a few yards of them.

As Hero contemplated all of this, he was looking down at the ground. A breeze brushed across his shoulders and blew his hair forward. Hero's head jerked toward the sky in reaction to the breeze and he noticed the sun had gone. The sky had returned to its charcoal color and the ominous darkness began to encroach itself across the river valley. *Jack!* Hero screamed. *He must've gotten out of the cave! How could I be so stupid as to leave him?* Hero sprinted as fast as his legs could carry him back to the cave. Over the boulders he leapt, as if they were not even there.

He barely crunched a stick or leaf as he ran with all his might back to the cave. His feet merely danced across the forest floor and Jack was his only thought.

As he approached the cave, Hero leapt straight from the ground hard to the right and pounced off the trunk of a tree which landed him halfway up the bluff. Hero pulled his knife from the sheath strapped to his leg and placed the blade in his mouth so as to use both hands to climb. Up the bluff he went, like a snow leopard climbing quickly to its den. At the mouth of the cave, Hero jumped in and rolled over his shoulder landing perfectly in a crouched defensive position, knife back in his right hand and left arm extended for balance.

Jack sat on the cot reading a book. He looked over at Hero and laughed. "You practicing for the apocalypse, Hero?"

I thought...

"That might be your problem, Hero. You think too much."

Hero was not amused at all by Jack's making fun of the situation. Nor, did the situation feel right at all. But Hero had nothing he could prove. There was Jack, sitting right where he left him. He would've had no strength to make the climb in the amount of time Hero was gone unless the Shadow helped him. The Shadow didn't appear to be present, though. But, Hero still wondered, *Why all the dark clouds and the breeze?*

Jack could understand his thoughts to an extent and offered his devious consolation. "Hero, if you're going to kill me every time a cloud rolls in or a breeze picks up you might as well get it over with now." Jack laughed at him and Hero could do nothing but sulk on the outside. On the inside, he remained suspicious.

As the night fell, the whispering of crickets and the screaming cicadas were a welcoming sign of spring to Hero. The increasing trickle inside the cave meant that spring rains would drive them out to the mouth again if they had to stay much longer. Jack lay in the back of the cave and something told Hero to tie him back up. Something just did not seem right to him. There was a reason for the sudden weather change. The animals were speaking outside, louder than they had at any other recent time. It was all very confusing to Hero. He was certain that if he tied Jack up, it would be a long time again to regain his trust and Hero did not want to have to walk that trail again, if at all possible. *I'll sleep with one eye open tonight and see how he is in the morning.*

From back in the cave Jack's eyes were wide open with excitement. His fingers trembled with power. The gun stuck intrusively in his back. But he did not mind. It was to be his saving grace. Hero would not touch a gun. Jack knew this; and he knew this is how he could be free. He was ready to act now!

No! You stupid worthless kid! You're going to wait until you are stronger. Convince him to let you go and then you can kill him!

The Shadow spoke strong in Jack's mind.

I want to be free now, though! Jack said to the Shadow.

You're only as free as I will let you be. That is the way it is, Jack! If you want out of this cave you better listen to me!

Jack's heart sunk a little. At times he didn't know if he should trust the Shadow or Hero. It was all mixed up in his head. The Shadow was hateful to him. But, the Shadow gave him strength and Hero tied him up and fed him only enough to stay alive.

Jack, we will get through this. I am going to keep you safe and make you strong. I am going to give you power over it all, Jack. I just need you to carry me a little further, Son.

CHAPTER TWELVE

Farron stumbled into the darkened doors of the Ragweed Bar in The Bluff. The floors were tile, green and what once was white, now yellowed from years of thick smoke and foot traffic. The jukebox played something silly, for which he was in no mood. Farron used his big clumsy arms to guide his way through the tables and chairs, drunk and stumbling. He meandered along through the maze of hindering objects until he found a lonely back table with as little of the blinding neon light as possible. His clothes were drenched in sweat and booze. He had urinated on himself the night before and his stench was repulsive to the only other two people that sat in the bar. They got up and made their way to the door. The bartender unleashed upon him, which was nothing new to Farron.

"Farron, either take a goddamn bath or stop coming in here!" she screamed.

"Alrighty, you sh... sh... shut your damn mouth, woman!"

Farron didn't even remember how he arrived here. His head was spinning uncontrollably. It had been one long night after the other that had turned into weeks and months of chasing the next drink. He had tried, time and time again to stop. But in the evening, it called his name and he inevitably went out and found it. Once he drank, there was no stopping. He drank all he could until he passed out, every night. His family was long gone. They had written him off as a bad decision, a bad husband and a bad father.

The barmaid grabbed Farron by his big left arm and pulled him out of the seat. He hit the dirty tile floor hard and lay there, not moving. He threw up the beer that he had not yet digested and the barmaid kicked him square in the back. Farron let out his breath in a grunt.

"Get the hell outa here, Farron! You ran off my only tips tonight!" She was a harsh woman. But you had to be harsh to put up with drunks all night. Sometimes that was the only language they understood.

Farron wouldn't move. The barmaid walked around the bar, cursing him more and angrily picked up the phone. She dialed the police and dispatch answered. Shortly after, three police cars showed up in the parking lot, their blue and red lights flooding every corner with the ambiance that runs off criminals as well as good paying patrons in the bar business. But it had to happen. Everywhere Farron showed up, people left, to never come back. He was a horrible sight to see these days.

Farron was still in the bar where the police found him lying under the table at which he had just been sitting. He was curled up around the base of it. His shirt and overalls were covered in the beer he had thrown up only a moment ago. His vomit was warm and filled the air with a stench. His legs were wet again with urine. One of the officers left with a remark to the other three about "rookies" and having to "sometimes get your hands dirty". He laughed as he left the bar. The other three began to lift Farron, two on his arms and one at his boots. It was a big job getting him to the door and they were exhausted by the time they made it to the parking lot.

It was warm out now, even in the evenings. The cold days of winter were over. The city police only had to deal with the real hardcore drunks like Farron, for the most part. Most of the other trouble was found in rural back yards or near the rivers in the county. The warm weather drove everyone out of the city to play. During the winter, the people would crowd the bars, and the city's officers had their work cut out for them. It was easy to obtain an abrasive personality when the only time you see the public is at their worst. This usually carried over to the drunks in the summertime and they were often treated terribly, no matter how much they may have "deserved it".

The tired cops dropped Farron on the asphalt with a thud. They stood there, bent over and panting. "This is bullshit, man! I could put a round in this one and make the world a better freaking place!" One said to the others. The other two agreed and began to reach down to give it another try.

Immediately, Farron began to convulse. "What the….!" Farron made gurgling sounds in the back of his throat. His eyes rolled back in his head and froth formed around his mouth and trickled down into his red beard. He shook uncontrollably and began to bleed out of his nose. "I didn't drop him that hard man!" The police radioed an ambulance which showed up shortly after.

When the paramedics arrived, they moved slowly. They thought, *What's the hurry? Another un-insured idiot off the map…* One of the ambulance drivers knelt low over Farron's face and spoke to him, "Hey ass-hole! Can you hear me? Are you dead or just dying?" They all laughed and removed the stretcher from the back of the ambulance. "He's still gotta pulse. Shoot him and write a report or take him in," said another. They loaded the big drunk man up on the stretcher and slung him in the ambulance.

The drive was slow. Farron was in and out of consciousness as they went along. He heard some of their jeers. But he was unable to react. He knew in the back of his mind that if he wanted any kind of care, the best thing to do was to keep his mouth shut. The last thing Farron remembered before slipping into long-sweet unconsciousness was the overhead light in the parking bay of the hospital.

****

It wasn't long before Farron was back with Jack at the ranch. He sat with the boy at the truck. The boy took his gun and Farron wanted it back. "Give it back, you little shit!"

"No, Farron!" Jack's voice was that of a child's. "Give it back!"

"I know what you want with it Farron!   Farron the fairy! Hah Ha Hah!" The boy laughed at him.

Farron reached in hard for the pistol and grabbed it from Jack. They struggled and fell to the ground, rolling across the grass, pushing and pulling against the firearm. BANG! The gun went off. Jack immediately fell back to the ground. Within a few seconds, blood began pouring from both sides of his mouth. His lips puckered like a fish out of water and his eyes glazed, staring into the distance. The color left his cheeks and the expression on his young face begged, "Why?" Then the boy's face changed. It was his own boy that lay there crumpled in the wet grass. Tears welled in Farron's eyes and terror crept upon him.

He fell to his knees and roared in his despair. He had murdered his child. He had torn his family asunder by his own selfishness and neglect. There was only a simple decision to make and it was done. Farron raised the .380 pistol to his temple, kneeling over his dead son. Then sand fell lightly from the gun onto his shoulder. In all his despair, he couldn't help but wonder where the sand had come from. Never mind. Farron pulled the trigger and fell to the ground, his vision turning to red and then black. Then a river flowed in the distance. Farron knew in his last desperate moments, that the rushing river must be the sound of the blood gushing out of his ears. The bullet had done its job and the world could finally be rid of him.

****

Farron awoke startled but unable to move. He was lying on his back and felt naked. There were tubes coming out of every hole in his body. He was confused. For a moment, he thought he had not killed himself successfully and then remembered that he had been having that dream for a while, now. He twisted on the hospital bed and saw men and women walking the hall. He tried to yell but the tube would not let him. Then the alarms went off.

"Farron! Farron! Calm down! You're going to feel a little pinch in your hip and then you need to relax!" The nurses were with him. A tear came back to his eye. His only thought at this point was, *Why did they let me live?* The drugs coursed through his veins and Farron could not help but relax. His eyes grew heavy and the room began to spin uncontrollably. The voices of the nurses all ran together into a monotone drone of sound and then... Silence, sleep, peace. No nightmares returned until he would wake again and realize that his life was to somehow continue on.

****

Before he could open his eyes, Farron heard the clattering of the food tray being rolled into his room. He wasn't hungry. Regardless, he still managed to open one eye and then the other. His entire body hurt; his head throbbed like it had never before. The tube in his throat was removed. His catheter had not, yet. There was still an intravenous drip in his arm and the heart monitoring pads still stuck to his chest. He wanted them off. But he hurt too badly to put up the fuss.

"You hungry, Mister Farron?" A sweet voice came from the other side of his bed.

"No." Said Farron

"Well, I'm going to at least leave some toast and apple juice here. I know you'd love to have some juice."

"You couldn't spare a shot of something in that juice could ya?"

"You, stupid man! That's what got you in here and now you're asking for it again! Why don't you just ask for a gun, Farron! It'd do ya about as much good!"

"Maybe I will!" he screamed back at her.

The on duty, doctor heard the commotion and entered the room. "Amy, what are you thinking? You cannot speak to a patient that way!"

"I'm sorry sir! He just got in here two nights ago from alcohol poisoning and he's asking for a drink!"

"Well, there are other ways to handle that, Amy. I think you need to move on from here and find some other employment."

"But, sir, I really love this job. Can I please have another chance? I'll apologize to Farron."

"The hell you will!" Farron spoke up. "I needed to hear that doc! You gotta pistol on your hands and she's a good one! If she leaves, I'm walkin' outa here too!"

"Farron, that's against my orders and Amy, your fired." The doctor's mind was made up.

Amy pushed the cart back to the nurse's station and shamefully asked one of her former co-workers to please take it back to the kitchen. They obliged and Amy began the long walk down the halls of the hospital. It is times like these that you tend to run into all the wrong people and it was the same for Amy. It seemed that no matter how fast she cleared the hallway, the news of what had happened in Farron's room stayed directly in front of her. Everyone she passed looked at her with pity and Amy felt terrible. She walked hard and fast, trying to outrun the news of her termination and erratic behavior. Finally, the exit appeared. She tried to push the doors open to the exit of the hospital only to remember that they opened on their own. She fell out onto the sidewalk, her arms grazing the dirty concrete, almost immediately drawing blood from the scrapes.

She could do nothing but sit there and cry. In all of her shame and embarrassment the people stepped around and over her, not even offering a hand to help her stand until Farron came from behind her and grasped her left shoulder. She jerked away and cursed him. He reached again and this time she let the big man help her up.

"I've had a bad day too, Sis. You wanna come sit down over here and lets us talk 'bout it?" Amy cracked the slightest of a broken smile through her utter despair and in her true form, agreed to sit with the man when most young women would have darted away with any excuse they could muster. They found a bench in a little smoker's shack about one hundred and fifty feet away from the hospital entrance. Farron asked Amy, "Do ya smoke, Sis?"

"I'm tryin' to quit."

"I didn't ask what you was tryin' to do. I asked if ya wanted a smoke."

"Right now, Mister Farron that would be amazing."

Farron looked across the smoker's shack and on the other side of it, he saw two teenage boys having a smoke and thumbing through the pictures of a magazine. He approached them.

"Hey fellas, could ya spare a smoke for my friend over here." Farron asked as friendly as he could. The boys never even looked up at him. Their eyes were fixed inappropriately, on Amy

"Who the hell are you, her daddy? Why don't she come ask us?"

Farron's friendly face changed to a hard stone-like grimace. "How 'bout you give up that magazine and the whole goddamn pack of smokes and I won't chew you up and shit you out on your momma's doorstep?"

The boys looked up at Farron and it was as if they kept looking up and up. They quickly gave up the magazine and two un-opened packs of cigarettes and darted off down the busy street. Farron had a way with people and his size usually gained him respect. The drink was his weakness, though. He was a good man and a loyal friend, if he could only stay sober. Amy giggled at his antics and graciously accepted the cigarette. Farron, being the gentleman, lit it for her and then lit one for himself. They sat back and just enjoyed the peace and quiet in the little shack that seemed to shield them from the sounds of the city.

"So, Farron where are you from, man?"

"Oh, I live here I guess. I used to live over around Two Rivers. But, me and the wife didn't see eye to eye."

"I hate to hear that." Amy replied

"What about you, Sis?"

"I'm an Okie. But I have been traveling around this way a little. A boy I met turned me on to this area and I ended up taking a job at the hospital a few weeks ago."

"Well, that didn't last long, huh?"

They both laughed at the bad humor. Amy liked Farron and he liked her as well. They sat in the smoker's shack and talked for several hours about their lives and how they came to sitting right there in that moment. Farron told Amy he was homeless and that he had been struggling with his drinking ever since he lost his son in an accident. Amy listened intently and her heart poured out to him. Amy was different than many young girls her age. Farron knew this. Many girls would have looked for any opportunity to walk away from him. But Amy actually seemed to enjoy their conversation. He was careful not to mistake her kindness for naiveté', however. The girl was anything but naive. She seemed wise beyond her years. Farron wondered how she came to be so. But, he wasn't comfortable asking that question. So, he let it be.

"Farron, do you have anywhere to stay?"

"No, Sis. I do not. But don't worry about that. I'll figure out something. This old man don't require a lot."

"Well, good. 'Cause I don't have a lot to offer you. But I do have a clean couch at my apartment. I cannot let you drink and if I catch you drinking, you're out right away. But I can't leave you out here all alone."

"Amy, that's not necessary."

"I didn't ask you if it was necessary, Mister Farron. I told you to come stay on my couch until you get your head cleared up."

Farron caught the obvious play on his own earlier words and chuckled at her. He agreed to stay with Amy for a few days. But he made no guarantees with regard to the drinking and accepted his fate if he was to be caught in the act. They stood up off the bench and began the walk to Amy's little red Honda.

Chapter Thirteen

Farron walked through the door of Amy's small apartment. It was humble, to say the least. Seated behind a seedy motel in The Bluff, it was only an extra building, owned by the motel. In the building, there appeared to be four small efficiency apartments. Amy's was on the top floor, far to the right. The building had the old plaster walls outside, painted white and each apartment was adorned with a lime green door and a matching set of shutters that stood out brightly on each side of the tenant's one living room window.

The living room was dimly lit by a cheap floor lamp. Farron imagined that Amy had probably drug that floor lamp everywhere with her. It looked as if it had seen better days. True to her word, a couch sat in the middle of the room adjacent to a little television stand, on which sat a small nineteen inch TV with a VCR on top of it. There was little else in the room, save a few books stacked in the corner beside what looked like a short "on the floor" version of an arm-chair. It was red, did not match anything in the apartment, and Farron thought it looked terribly uncomfortable.

"Have a seat on the couch and I'll be back in a moment with a blanket and pillow." Said Amy

Farron did as he was told and sat on the little couch, making it creak under his weight. He worried that he might break it and thought maybe he should just sleep on the floor.

Moments later, Amy bounced back into the living room and threw a blanket and pillow down on the couch. "There ya go, Mister Farron. You're all set."

"Amy, you can just call me Farron. We're not at the hospital anymore."

"I like calling you Mister Farron. It's kinda cute and it sets a nice healthy boundary between our ages, don't ya think?" Amy said without missing a beat.

"Sure, Sis."

Farron couldn't disagree with that no matter how he tried. Many things Amy said were like that. She had a way of speaking with which one could not disagree. She was beautiful, quirky, far too young for Farron and smart as a whip. He liked her a lot. He wondered why anyone wouldn't like her, which brought him to the obvious question. Where was her husband or the boyfriend? Better yet, where was her father, her brother, her mother and sister? Farron did not know if it was appropriate to ask. So he kept the question to himself. Although he assumed her answer would probably be just as quick and quaint as was everything else she said.

One thing was for sure. Amy approached life like few others. She went in with an open mind, an honest opinion and no fear. In fact, Farron thought, *she's full of.... What was that thing? She's full... of ... love. That was it. She brought me here. She let a homeless drunk, twice her age, sleep on her couch. She lost her job for telling a desperate patient the truth. So far, that was what Farron thought of her. She must actually be full of love. What a rare quality!*

"Farron, the bathroom is down the hall to the right. I poured the mouthwash down the sink. So, there won't be any drinking tonight, unless you want me to make you a cup of coffee."

Farron took a small offense to the remark, at first. But he soon accepted that he would have drunk it if it was available. He wondered where a young girl would have learned the tricks of the alcoholic trade. This time he asked.

"Sis, where'd you learn about that?"

"Oh, the mouthwash trick; I read about it! Did you know that alcoholics are usually some of the most emotionally driven people that exist? They can be amazing innovators and very influential people. But, left to their own devices, they... I think the book said 'pull the walls down around themselves', or something like that."

"Sounds like a good book. I think that's the nicest thing anybody has ever said about me."

"So you're admitting it? Congratulations, Mister Farron! That's the first step!"

"I'm not admitting nothing! I just said it was a nice thing to say."

Amy decided it wasn't a battle to fight and pushed his big head down on the arm of the couch. "Get some sleep, Mister Farron. I'll make breakfast in the morning." Amy shut the floor lamp off and left the living room. The darkness brought on the loneliness to which Farron was very accustomed. He lay there alone and the same need of each night set in quickly. Farron knew the only thing to quench it was a drink. He took a few deep breaths and thought about it for a moment. He really wanted to see Amy in the morning and he knew she would lock her door if he left. That was the deal. Farron decided to just sweat it out for one night and told himself that maybe he could talk her in to letting him have a drink tomorrow. He knew in his heart that she wasn't that gullible. But, it was the only way to shut his mind down for the time being. Farron hadn't gone a night without drinking in years. In fact, he couldn't even remember when that was. He just knew it had to have been years.

Hours passed in the darkness before sleep would come to Farron. He was hot and then cold, sweating and then shivering. The blanket was kicked off time and time again. The pillow was beaten to a pulp and Farron tossed and turned until at least three o' clock in the morning. Finally, a light sleep over-took him and he began to breathe deeply.

****

He fell to his knees and roared in his despair. He had murdered his child. He had torn his family asunder by his own selfishness and neglect. There was only a simple decision to make and it was done. Farron raised the .380 pistol to his temple, kneeling over his dead son. Then sand fell lightly from the gun onto his shoulder.

****

"Farron! Mister Farron! Wake up! You're having a nightmare!" Farron shot up off the couch and fell into the floor with a crash.

"What? What the...?"

"Mister Farron, are you alright?"

"I need a drink, Amy!" Farron shouted, still half asleep.

"Let's just sit up and talk for a bit, Mister Farron. It's almost five in the morning anyway. Let's just go ahead and start this day right. You sit there and I'll be right back with a cup of coffee for ya. Sound good?"

"I said I want a drink, girl! I don't want no damn coffee!"

"Farron, I might remind you that you are in my home. I will let that kind of disrespect fly once. But, I will not do it again." She spoke sternly, but softly.

Farron sighed and rubbed his eyes. "I am sorry. I'll give the coffee a try."

Farron sat back up on the couch and flung the blanket back to the floor. He was burning up. He couldn't imagine drinking something hot. But, at least he would be drinking something. His body was starved for sugar and yelled into the kitchen to Amy.

"Mind dumpin' some sugar in mine?"

"I already did, hun."

"Thank ya, Sis."

About ten minutes later, Amy returned with two cups of hot coffee and sat next to Farron on the couch. She noticed his hands were trembling and tried not to pay too much attention to it to keep from embarrassing to him. She placed the cup in his hands and Farron immediately spilled it over the edge and onto the couch.

"Damnit Farron!" He cursed himself, all the while spilling more, not being able to control his trembling hands.

"Amy, I am so sorry."

"Farron, why don't we go sit down in the kitchen? You can lay the coffee cup on the table so it doesn't jitter so badly." Amy felt terribly sorry for his pain. She took his cup and Farron followed her into the kitchen.

It was equally as mismatched and bare as the living room, with yellow painted walls from floor to ceiling and dirty white cabinets. There was a stove and oven. The dishes were piled high in the sink and a coffee maker sat in the corner, steaming with the fresh made brew. They sat and sipped the coffee, at first, in silence. Amy broke it, not too much later.

"What's your nightmare about mister Farron?"

"It's weird. Why do you ask, Sis?"

"I heard somewhere that if you talk about what is torturing you, it shows itself less in your dreams. I don't know if it is true. But we can give it a try."

Farron would normally shrink away from this type of intrusive conversation. But Amy's personality made Farron feel safe enough to get a little bit off his chest. He opened up to her, very slowly and cautiously, watching her facial expressions. The first sight of shock and he planned on stopping. He felt there was no need to ruin such a great young girl with the horrible stories and nightmares of his life. Amy sat and listened intently.

"Well, about eight months ago, I gave this kid a ride to some ranch he wanted to visit. Good looking kid, he was. I picked him up at the new Willow Junction. By the time I got him to the ranch, I was trashed and passed out in the yard of the place, there. When I picked the kid up, everything seemed alright. But, the next morning, when he woke me, everything was wrong. The kid didn't even look like himself anymore. I figured I was just too drunk to recognize him. He had my gun. He had taken it from me the night before. Like I said, smart kid. Anyway, he tried to give it back, seein' that I had sobered up and what not. But, as soon as my hands touched..." Farron paused for some time.

"Go ahead Mister Farron. It's alright", said Amy.

"As soon as my hand touched it, I knew I had to kill him." Farron hung his head in despair.

"Something was telling me this kid was possessed or something. I started to turn the gun toward my own head. That's how real it was. I thought I'd off my worthless self before I ever hurt that poor kid."

"What did you do?" Amy asked with genuine worry in her voice.

"I give him the gun. He tried to give it back, which was going to turn into a fight. So I sped away. But in the dream, I don't speed away. We fight over the gun and it goes off. It shoots the boy and he dies somethin' awful right there in front of me. Then his face changes." Farron's words broke to tears.

"He changes... into my... my boy, that I lost. Then I turn the gun on myself and sand falls out of it. But, it still works, I think, except that I keep wakin' up. I worry everyday about givin' that boy that gun. I never should have. Somethin' was wrong with him. He was off his rocker, somehow or 'nother."

A short time went by in silence. Amy hung her head low and Farron wondered to himself if he had just bought himself a one way ticket out of her good graces. He thought she must think him deranged to have had such a crazy dream. *She'll probably kick you out now, dumbass! When do they start sellin' liquor? I guess if she does, I can get me a drink.*

"You'll do no such thing, Farron." Amy said aloud.

"Do what? How did you? How did you do that?"

"Where did you drop off Jack, Farron?" Amy asked.

"Hey that was his name! You know him?"

Again, Amy asked sharply, "Do you remember where you dropped him?"

"Yeah, it was somewhere around Birch Creek."

"Could you direct me there?"

"I reckon, Sis, if I had to. Why?

" 'Cause, we have to go get him." Amy said somberly.

Chapter Fourteen

The morning was already hot. Jack had had all of it he would take. The cave grew smaller each day. He had become the master of disguising the Shadow that lived proudly inside him. He protected it with the integrity of a soldier and disguised it as well as any Russian spy. He used the last month to hone his expertise and he worked hard on Hero as well. He tried to be as needy as possible, asking Hero to get this and that, always appearing to need whatever it may be as desperately as possible and seemingly forever grateful for Hero's service. The plan was working well. Hero ran to his bidding to keep him alive. When Hero was gone, Jack flung into action, strengthening his body and his mind. He listened intently to the Shadow each step of the way.

Each night, Hero returned to their camp in the cave, more and more weary, exhausted and beaten down by the hard bluffs, the sweltering temperatures and the ruthless work that Jack had him do. Hero had only seen Eli and Janice once during all of this time. Eli warned him not to let Jack become stronger.

Eli, I have to get him out of that cave. The Shadow is nowhere to be seen. He is Jack again. A little fine tuning and we will be as right as rain.

"Hero, the Shadow is never gone. You should've learned that in the battle." said Eli

Maybe I am that good, Eli. Maybe I got rid of it all together.

Hero knew better than to think like this. But as his name suggests, Hero had an ego that he had to have help controlling. All of this time alone and Jack had only inflated it with his constant gratitude, however false it may have been. Hero had worked himself to exhaustion to feed his hungry ego. They had begun to dangerously feed off of one another. Hero could not see it all. He was blind to the entire event as it unfolded before him. But Jack and the Shadow were well aware. They had nearly become one. The Shadow didn't have to give Jack instructions as it did before. It only had to continuously support him, converse and praise his every decision as they were all in the Shadow's service at this point.

It was nearly nine o' clock in the morning. Jack lay obediently in his cot planning the day as it would unfold. Hero sat at the mouth of the cave, crouched and staring sternly out over the river valley. The sun was out and cooking the earth. The river flowed wild and the birds sang loudly. Squirrels were alive in the trees chirping their warnings and a deer walked cautiously, one step at a time, below him on the leafy forest floor. The sun's rays broke through the canopy overhead and shone on the doe. Her head twitched upward and her left eye sparkled in the sun. Hero did not move an inch. He stayed crouched like a good hunter, strong and still.

Jack crouched directly behind him, holding his breath. Hero had not heard Jack move at all. He was able to get off the cot and move slowly across the rocky floor of the cave without alerting Hero.

It is time, my son. Not here. But today is the time. You are ready.

The doe looked back down to the earth and continued her steps forward, nose down for any fresh vegetation to eat. As she moved about fifty more feet away, Hero began his careful, quiet descent from the bluff. He moved in unison with the swaying trees, careful to make no more sound than the loudest squirrel overhead. Every step was a meticulous calculation of chance and Hero was the master of the game, without a gun. The doe went out of sight.

"There she went, Hero!" Jack screamed at the top of his lungs. Hero spun suddenly. Jack was pointing up river to a clearing. Something shone bright in the small of his back. "She ran to the field!" Jack jumped from the mouth of the cave and scaled the bluff with amazing precision. Hero was amazed and taken aback by his ability. But Jack didn't give him much time to think. Jack darted past him at a cheetah's pace.

Jack Stop! Hero knew something was wrong. He shouldn't be that strong.

The forest was alive. It was more alive than it should've ever been. The sun shone far too bright. The trees swayed wildly with the wind. Every bird, every squirrel, every insect screamed with wild excitement and confusion. Leaves were kicked up with fierce power and swirled in the air. Hero was weak, too weak to give chase. But Jack was his responsibility. Hero lurched forward and ran with all he had after Jack.

Hero leapt over each boulder and downed tree. His feet slammed hard against the earth. He shed his bow and quiver of arrows in mid run to save weight. The mission was no longer to kill the deer. Now it was to get Jack back to the cave. He ran across the small trail down to the river and heard splashing. Jack was crossing the river. Hero made a hard right ninety degree turn and headed straight for the water. He went in with a splash. The river had risen several feet with no recent rain and whipped wildly down its grade with a strong current that knocked Hero off his feet.

After gaining his foothold on a rock at the bottom, Hero began to swim as hard as he could across the swirling torrent of cold water. The sandy bank couldn't come quick enough and by the time it did, Hero planted his body against it panting and struggling for each breath. The sun was burning his skin as it amplified with each of Jack's steps away from him. *C'mon Hero; Just push through and get to him. You can do this!*

Hero used all the strength in his waning body to lift himself up off the bank and trudge forward after Jack. The briars pulled at his clothes and his skin. He tore through them not paying any attention to the pain, the blood now trickling down his legs. Every step was a throwing of his body forward and catching himself with the next step. His energy was obliterated and he pushed off of each tree and fell to the earth again and again until he finally reached the edge of the field.

"Right here, Hero. Just a little further." said Jack. He stepped out from behind a large cottonwood tree. Hero, on his hands and knees looked up. There Jack stood, all of his color back, not even panting after the run. "I've outsmarted the forest, the animals and even you, you poor son of a bitch! They don't even know I am here, yet! But they will, Hero! They're gonna know all about me when I am done."

What do you plan on accomplishing, Jack? Hero said, between struggling gasps for air.

"Accomplishing? You think I am here to accomplish something?"

We're all here to accomplish something, Jack.

"My job is to simply be, Hero. I'm going to be bigger than you. My job is to consume. I consume it all and I become it all and it all depends on me!"

You're lost, brother.

"I am not your brother, Hero! I am not you!"

Jack pulled the gun from his waist and leveled it down to Hero's sternum, covered only by a white cotton shirt he rarely ever wore. "It isn't going to jam up this time, Hero! You're done!"

Hero stood helpless and exhausted. There was nothing he could see to do but accept his fate. There was no way of talking Jack down. He was consumed by the Shadow. Hero wondered how he could've been so silly as to lose sight and be tricked by Jack. But, he knew this wasn't really Jack. This was Jack controlled by something else. Hero could have been the controlling force just as well. Sure, it was up to Jack to choose. But, Hero knew if he had been more prepared, more adept, more able; he could have saved Jack. He felt that this was his failure as much as it was Jack's. Hero felt that he might as well have been holding the gun on himself. He had done it just as much as Jack had. They were one, just as Jack and the Shadow were one. Everything depended on the other to bring them all to this point, this terrible climax of murderous reality, in which Hero must die at the hand of his enemy, his brother and his self.

The gun fired with a quick flash and all was silent except the droning whistle of the lead hurling through the air and sinking deep into Hero's chest. He was blown back off his feet and landed on his back. His breath was immediately knocked out and his body lurched for air; but there was none to be had for a moment. When it did come back, it was like breathing through a straw that was continuously dunked in water; but the water wasn't water at all. Hero was breathing his own blood.

Jack walked past him and never gave Hero another look before calmly stepping back into the dense forest. He headed back to their camp at the cave.

Hero struggled to stand. He fell twice before he eventually mustered the strength to get up. He hoped for a breeze in the field and stepped into it, out of the forest. There was a large tree ahead. If he could make the tree's shade, he could get the breeze and the shade all in one. He would also be more visible for help if someone was within eyesight. He knew it was a longshot. But, anything was better than to die, not having tried. Hero focused on the tree and began his steps in that direction. The heat bore down on him and cooked his skin. The wind dried his once wet clothing and all that soaked him now was his own blood.

Hero fell hard on the dry grass like a heavy feed sack. The thud of his fall, he felt deep in his bones. The ache burned and throbbed and every pore screamed for relief. He used his waning twisted muscles to slowly turn his head around. He wondered how far he would have to pull himself to get the relief that only the cool shade could offer under the tree. It was still at least thirty feet. It would be thirty feet of painful torture to get any respite from the grueling sun. It was thirty feet too many. Hero couldn't muster the strength to move another inch. He had managed to slow the blood earlier when he tried to rest. He had tried clotting it with his once white t-shirt. But, in his panicky race to get somewhere, anywhere, he was pumping blood like a coughing spicket from his broken sternum. His shirt was fruitless as good clotting material. It was full of fresh warm blood, enough to be rung out.

Somehow, being shot always seemed an honorable death. The movies he had seen displayed it proudly, the good guy laying in the street bleeding out his heart and bleeding his last goodbyes from a stiff lip to the beautiful lady holding his head as she cried for him. This felt anything but honorable. There were no beautiful women to hold his head. The only things he could utter were bloody gurgling moans and salty, lonely tears. Desperate fear filled every cell of his being. *What a stupid thing to say!* He thought. *Honorable death! What death is honorable?*

He lay there, panting every breath. He was exuding precious moisture and energy from his body and couldn't control it. *This is it. This is the sum of my life.* He thought of all the people he had met. He wondered if they might be thinking of him in this instance. *Did I leave them with a happy thought of me or are they angry by anything I may have done? Are they thinking, 'That crazy boy! What an idiot!' Or have I lived up to my name? Am I a Hero?*

The bright sun had shrouded itself with a dark cloak and now showed itself as a shrinking point of light in his eyes only. His breaths grew shallow. His body still heaved in the futile attempt to breathe precious air. His back arched and his fingers clenched upon themselves in the throes of death. Smaller and smaller, the point of light slipped away and the breathing halted abruptly. No more sight. No more sensations of touch save a faint tingle in his feet. His body could not move. His muscles were rigid and useless. For the first time in his life, he recognized and felt his own brainwaves coursing in a frantic rush to save his life. They were electricity channeling through his head. They moved like pinballs at the speed of lightning. But they could find no hole in which to sink and rest, and affect the nervous system. He had never been more aware than in this moment of his functioning mind. It is strange that only in dis-function do we ever really realize how we functioned before. It was to no avail. A final dry exhale was his only goodbye. It was his last words of love. That lonely breath outward toward the ether, from whence he came was Hero's final call to the life that he left behind. Hero passed on.

CHAPTER FIFTEEN

Jack walked back to the cave. His thoughts wandered a bit. The darkness crept about him. The forest lay still and quieted more and more with each passing moment. The river slowed and the birds began to fly away. Soon he could hear nothing but his footsteps in the crunching leaves. When he arrived at the bank of the river, he looked down expecting to swim across as he had before. But it was not so this time. Jack stepped into the slow moving water and walked slowly all the way across. By the time he reached the other side, he spoke out loud. "What now Shadow?"

Stay with me Jack and everything will be provided from here on out. Jack trusted the entity and walked on.

By the time he arrived at the cave, the river had gone stagnant. The wind blew again at the old ominous speed that blew the leaves in the same rattling way that nearly drove him mad. The Shadow was inside him before. But now, it felt as if he was following the Shadow's every move. He was doing what he was told by the Shadow in every moment.

The thought crossed his mind, *Have I made a mistake?*

Jack, pull it together! We do this together, you and me! Stop asking the crazy questions!

Jack apologized and put his mind back on track.

Once at the base of the bluff, he began the climb upward, scaling the rocky face, one crevice at a time. He tired more quickly than he should have. He didn't have near the energy that he had before. Once at the top, Jack gathered a little wood and lit himself a fire to ward off the encroaching dark.

What's with all the damn light, Jack! Screeched the Shadow.

"I just want to see some light! What's the big deal with that?" The Shadow brought up a wind and blew it out.

Jack, trust me when I tell you that we need to lay low for a little while. Jack didn't understand; but he let the Shadow have his way.

Jack crawled across the floor of the cave in the darkness until he found the cot and curled up on it. Something felt wrong. He felt like he had been tricked. *What am I left with here?* It seemed terribly one-sided. It seemed as if he had been a chess piece in someone else's game. The realization that he had been used set in deeply and Jack sobbed in the cot alone. He was absolutely alone like he never had been before.

There was no desire to consume anything or for anything to depend on him because the Hero wasn't there to challenge him anymore. *What can I combat? What can I fight? What do I have to admire? Nothing. There is nothing!*

****

Early in the morning, before the sun could even get the lost opportunity to shine, Jack found himself at the river's edge again, facing the field. The water behind him was as black as it had ever been and not a living thing thrived between its banks. His legs stung from the acidic quality of the water now. It tasted like brine on his skin. Not a frog croaked. Not a snake slithered. Jack's world was dead. His only hope was to lie in the field before him in what was possibly the last dew that Jack would ever see or feel on his bare feet.

As he approached Hero, lying in the grass, all he could see was that Hero was gone and only the broken body of a once resilient man lay crumpled in the dew, soaking it up.

Jack looked down at the man and thought, *It's all screwed up now.* He tilted his head back and fell to his knees. He looked up at the black sky. He beat his chest angrily and screamed with all of his might, "What have I done?... It is over now."

****

Amy and Farron bounced down the road in Amy's Red Honda. "Farron are you sure this is the way?"

"Sure I'm sure, Sis."

"Well, you were drunk the last time you were here, Farron."

"Yep, But I left sober as a judge."

Amy rolled her eyes a little and Farron laughed under his breath. Amy had tried several times to call the ranch phone that Jack had given her. But no one would answer it. She knew something must be wrong. If Jack had gotten a hold of the gun and the Shadow was with him, it would not be a good ending unless she could get there in time to help. She had tried to explain some of this to Farron on the way. But the more she explained, the more confused he became.

"Mister Farron you are going to learn a lot about how life works and all the important roles we play during the next little while."
"How long is a little while, Sis?"

"As long as it takes."

She explained, "You see Mister Farron, we are all made up of different desires and intentions. We all have different things that we want in life and we create characters to go get those things. Very few of us feel capable of going to get them ourselves because we often see ourselves as inadequate.

"Uh huh." Farron replied.

"Don't believe me? Alright. I bet you wanted to leave last night when you found out there was no chance of getting a drink at my house, didn't ya, Mister Farron."

"Well, yeah Sis. You're right about that. But the point is I didn't do it. I didn't want to think of you getting up in the morning and lookaying disappointed at your empty couch. I didn't want you to think that I had picked the bottle over you."

"Well, sure that was your motivation. Now tell me about the character that goes through with the good deed."

"Oh you mean like the angel and the devil on your shoulders, telling you right from wrong!"

"Well, sort of, Mister Farron. Except take out all your ideas of what is right and was is wrong and just think of it in terms of benefits and consequences. One action gives you a benefit, the other a consequence."

"Alright.", answered Farron. "Sis, I reckon my character is kind of a knight in shining armor sort o' fella."

"Most men's are." Amy responded. "Now tell me about him."

"Well, if I wanna get up and go take a drink or stop something I ought not do or even start something I oughta do, I just pretend to be the biggest baddest man alive and I make myself the courage and I go get it done."

"Kinda like when you got the cigarette, at the hospital?"

"Yeah, that!"

"Well, Mister Farron, I think you have found your character! Do you see what I am saying?"

"Yeah Sis, I see it as clear as mud!"

Amy smiled as they continued down the dirt road. Farron mentioned that the clouds must be rolling in because the further ahead they drove, the darker it got. Amy assured him it wasn't the clouds.

"So, Sis, one thing I don't get for sure...."

"What's that?"

"Well, where do you fit in to all of this? I mean all these characters are runnin' around fightin' amongst each other and somehow you know all about it. Not only that, you knew Jack! How do you know all this crazy stuff?"

"Mister Farron, I am another character. But I am a character that gets to represent lots of people. I get to show up all the time. A lot of times, here lately in this world I get beat out by other characters. But, if there was ever anybody that might let me fight for them, it would be you and Jack."

"What character are you, Amy?"

"I am Love."

Farron sat back in silence contemplating their conversation. He had been through quite a bit in the last few days. From his drunken stupor to the hospital, to Amy's couch and now he found himself out on some adventure with this girl, half his age. He didn't know what to make of it all. But it was fun. It was exciting and he wanted to continue. The one question that burned in his mind was, however, unanswered. It was his fault though. He had yet to ask it. He was afraid to hear the answer. He could think of no real good answer to the question he so longed to ask. But, Amy seemed forthright and open about her thoughts. She seemed kind. *Hell, she said she was "Love"!*

There was no way he actually believed she was some sort of unearthly entity. He just thought she meant that she tried to exemplify love in every situation. *Is that what she meant by that?* He asked himself. Then he thought, *Well, if that's the case, couldn't we all be love?* Farron's head was cloudy with thoughts, and he was excited to see that from the view out of the windshield, it appeared to him that they were getting close to the gates of the place where he had dropped off Jack.

"One last question, Amy; and then I'll leave ya alone."

"Ask me anything, Mister Farron."

"If you're "Love" and you're comin' out here to set something right, then what the hell am I? Drivin' Miss Daisy?"

Amy laughed. "No Mister Farron. You're my second choice."

"Well, by God I've been that before! But, I think we got off on the wrong damn foot."

Amy turned to him and put her soft hand on his big shoulder. She leveled her eyes into his and said, "Mister Farron you'd better start taking this very seriously. It isn't a joke. None of this is a game. There is a very good chance that Jack has murdered his Hero, the little thing that fights his hardest battles for him. I am going to ask that you step up and become the Hero if that is the case. Do you think you're up for that?"

"Well, hell no!" Farron yelled. "Jesus Christ. Girl! Here we are on mission to save the world and the Lord picked a drunk and a teeny bopper to do the job! I should've stayed drunk!"

Amy shot her eyes across the car and said, "You'll come around when the time is right. You can't help but protect what you love. I already know that about you, Mister Farron."

Farron sulked back in his seat as they continued down the path to the gates of the ranch. The darkness was everywhere. He was afraid and looking right to left for anything that he could see. He caught Amy in the corner of his eye. She had tears on her cheeks and he reached over to comfort her.

"Sis, I'm sorry. I'll take it more serious. I am here for ya. You know that don't ya?"

"Mister Farron, it's not what you said that I am crying over. It's what I know. This has gotten very bad and we've got quite a job on our hands."

Amy knew that something beautiful had died here today. Whatever it was, she was too late. It was done. The Shadow had taken control of this land and was consuming it at a pace that she had never seen before.

Chapter Sixteen

Eli heard the gravel crunch and grind under the tires of the vehicle as it meandered down the long driveway to the gate. He picked himself up off the ground and dusted a little of the dirt that clung to his pant legs. He walked in the circle shaped path around the berm of the sweat lodge to get to the walking path. This is the path leads back to his tree house. From there, he has an excellent vantage point to see who is traveling up the drive. He walked with is head down, not excited in the least over company, only curious and thinking of a way to shirk whomever it may be.

Eli was deep in his depression. He had not seen Janice in days. She stayed in the main house and did not come out. There was nothing beautiful to see. The wind blew constantly. Clouds hung over head and had for days. The wild animals were gone and the animals that they raised fended for themselves near the barns. There was a hard loneliness that had settled in the rolling hills that made up the once beautiful landscape of this mysterious land. The loneliness encroached upon every living thing it came into contact with and Eli and Janice were no exception.

They were overwhelmed by it; simple as that. They weren't possessed as was Jack. They were overtaken by its sadness. They were destroyed over Jack having succumbed to it and bringing such terror to the land he loved as much as they did. Hero was a man that Eli knew only by his existence and watched him fondly in many encounters with Jack over the years. However, the Shadow was ever present and Eli was woefully aware of him as well. The Shadow had permeated Jack's personality over the last several years. Eli read it in his letters. He saw it in him during the short visits he made while passing through. Eli had often wondered, *Did he pick this ghost up along the road somewhere? What had Jack seen that caused him to give the Shadow so much power? Was there any way to help him?*

Eli knew of none. He had invited Jack to the ranch one year ago and by the time he finally made it; the land predicted his coming long before he got there. It became gloomy even at the thought. In all of Jack's letters, he was in sort of a manic mood. Sometimes he would write as to how wonderful the open road was only to suddenly change his mood and express his disgust over the local people in whatever town he was in at the time. Many of his phone call were the same. At times, he was so upset, he would scream and yell at Eli or Janice over the phone and then seconds later, he would not remember it and be as cheerful as ever. Eli tried to talk to him and make some sense. But Jack would really never hear any of it.

"Eli, I'll be down in November and we'll talk about this then. Everything's fine, man. You just make sure there's fish in the river and work for me to do." That's all he would say.

Janice was reluctant to letting Jack stay due to the manic attitude he displayed. She had warned Eli that something wasn't quite right and that Eli should go to Jack himself, before bringing that energy to the land that they shared, especially since they were prone to share it with others as well. She made a very good point as Janice would often do. But Eli had a stubborn streak as well as his loving kindness, and felt sure that he could help Jack once he arrived. He also felt that Jack needed the land to heal.

Eli rounded the old bunkhouse and began walking down the drive toward the main house to meet the approaching car. The young girl was someone he was sure he had met and the big man, he had no clue of his identity. The little red car came to a stop next the front door of the main house and the two people stepped out.

"Janice doesn't like it when you park there." Eli said

"Where would you like us then, Eli?" replied Amy.

"Who are you guys and how do you know me, young lady?"

"We'll get to that, Eli. Just tell me where we should park."

Eli looked up the hill and pointed to the usual parking place above the bunkhouse.

"Just put it up there."

Farron stayed outside the car as Amy climbed back in and spun a little gravel in her attempt to climb the steep rocky hill. Both men felt awkward and didn't seem to know what to say to one another. Immediately, Farron wished he was back inside the car and getting out of here. He kicked at the ground and Eli just stared at him. Farron looked up at the windows of the main house and could see Janice looking back out at him, perplexed and irritated.

"Look man, I don't really know why we're here. All I know is that girl up there seems to be on a mission for some young man and she thinks I can help her."

"That young man is nothing she wants to get involved in right now, sir." Replied Eli

---

"Well you're going to have to tell her that, because I have tried and she listens about as well as any woman does."

Amy stepped carefully and gracefully back down the rugged hill to Eli and Farron. They were both looking at her like they had been caught with their "hands in the jar".

"Talking about me?"

"Only good stuff, I promise," said Farron

Eli, quietly exclaimed, "Who are you people?"

"I apologize sir! My name is Amy and this is my friend, Farron."

Eli took her hand reluctantly. "I would introduce myself. But it appears you already know who I am." Amy explained to Eli that she did and told him the story of picking up Jack and about them talking all the way from north of Big Spring to the old Junction. She told him a bit about meeting Farron and that Farron had actually dropped Jack off here some time ago. She asked if Jack was here at the ranch, even though she already knew he was just to see if Eli would lie to her. But he did not. He reported that Jack was at the ranch, but that he was not feeling well at all and probably didn't need to see anyone.

"You think you are the only one that can save him don't you."

"What?" Eli asked seemingly amazed at her presumptuous attitude.

"Eli, I am more than meets your eye here today. I know that I am familiar to you, as I should be."

"You are familiar. But I cannot place you."

"You have been through a lot, both you and Janice. I am here to help, Eli. Just think of me as a friend. I am not here to cause any more harm than it takes to help save you, Janice, your land, and your friend Jack from this Shadow. It is time we act and if we don't, Eli, it will have gone too far to come back. There already has been a lot of damage done. But I must believe it is repairable as must you."

"That sounds all well and good, Amy. Now, go convince Janice of that and maybe I can give you a try." Eli said in a sad and joking manner.

Amy asked where Janice was and Eli directed her to the door directly behind her at the front entrance of the Main House. She turned, took a few steps and twisted the old knob. The door sort of fell open as the house had settled many years prior. Amy stepped into the dim front room, lit only by the grey light that peaked through the dusty windows. The light was forced to creep over the hanging ferns that were dying slowly like everything else here. Old work boots sat in the corner along with tools that still had the previous summer's mud caked all over them.

Amy was only halfway through the threshold when she heard her friend speak up. "Sis, why don't I go in there with ya?" yelled Farron from the driveway.

Amy turned around and put her index finger to her lips telling Farron to be quiet. *This girl is loony going in there by herself.* "Eli this is crazy! I am not lettin' her go traipsing through someone else's home, uninvited!"

This adventure of saving people, he did not know much about and going into old houses that didn't look friendly seemed terribly scary to Farron. The whole atmosphere was gloomy and the big house loomed over him and this strange man in front of him. All of this and here went his only friend walking in by herself. *What was in there that caused Amy to tell me to keep quiet?*

Eli spoke softly to him. "Farron, I know I know her from somewhere and it just may be somewhere special. Let's give her a moment. If something goes wrong, we'll get her out of there."

Farron kept his eyes hard on the upstairs window where the woman was peering out at them. He could no longer see her there. But something did not seem right with her. He wondered why she wouldn't come out, at least to run them off.

Amy opened the second door that led into the big open foyer. It was dark. Not a light remained burning inside the house. Even less of the grey sunlight made it through the windows and over the dying plants. Amy looked toward the kitchen, first to see if the woman was present. Dirty dishes were piled high in the sink and across the counter, and clothes were strewn across the chairs. A French press with molded coffee sat on the kitchen bar to her right. Loose papers scattered across the floor blew up with the opening of the door. The cardboard planks that made up the interior walls stacked themselves ominously high to a ceiling of heavy despair, loathing Amy's presence and giving chase to her intentions. The house itself was on guard. It was aware that love was present and it stalked her like the rare cougars that lived within these Ozark hills. Amy took a step back and used the moment to control her breathing. She wanted to bring Farron inside to help her. But he didn't understand completely what was going on yet. So, she had to brave this one alone. She tried hard to leave Amy behind her and step into her own Hero, Love.

She closed her eyes and remembered her dream. She remembered everything she was and picked the highest version of herself that she could conceive. Amy accepted and transcended that version of herself and became it more and more with every breath she took.

When she opened her eyes, they were tearful and white. Fear no longer existed within her. The house cowered from her and she opened the door to the second floor. Up the stairs she walked. There was no need for her to call out Janice's name. Janice knew exactly where she was and would never acknowledge her presence until forced. Once upon the second floor, she knew this was Janice's favorite place. There were colorful blankets laying across a cream colored couch. Big bay windows looked over the fields outside to the south and all the way back to the Blue House that Jack had been dropped off at when this all began.

Things looked a little less awry up on this floor. It seemed Janice was not completely sucked up by her Shadow. However, she wasn't far from it and the Shadow was strong in presence here. It seemed she had been running from it. She had moved up here at some point and she hadn't gone downstairs in quite some time. There was one more floor up a ladder in a room adjacent to this main one. Love headed that way. She sensed Janice to be up there, hiding from her; doing what the Shadow told her to do. It was obvious to Amy that Janice had let the house become the portal for her own Shadow. The house embodied the Shadow. It pulsed with cold breath that sent chills down her spine. But she showed no fear outwardly. Janice had locked herself inside and given herself to it in nearly every way. She dared not come out and the Shadow was powerful enough now to threaten her if she even thought of leaving.

Amy placed her hand upon one of the lower rungs and began to climb. Her senses led her to the floor that Janice was on. She knew that there were several rooms that she left unchecked. Her gut told her Janice had climbed to the top to avoid her presence. It was no doubt to Amy that the Shadow told Janice to do so.

It was dead silent in the space above her head. It was dark and drafty and felt empty. This is where Amy's heart took her. Janice must be here. But there was not a sound at all to give her away. To go back down would be giving up; so Amy ascended the next rung of the wooden ladder. As her head crested the black opening above her, a shrill scream let out and Amy felt a hard blow to the side of her head from Janice's heel. It nearly knocked her from the ladder and stars circled in her vision. Her pain was excruciating. But she whipped around quickly to defend herself. Janice had been lying at the top directly above her in total silence waiting to attack on the orders of the Shadow. *She was here!* Amy knew it and had followed her heart straight to Janice! Amy grabbed the foot and pulled herself up by it. Janice lay at the top of the ladder waiting for her and gained only the one successful blow.

"Who are you and why are you here with us?" Janice screamed at her.

Amy straddled her and held her down. Janice kicked and swung as much as possible. But she was too weak for Amy. The Shadow had consumed her to the point of weakness. It would have been a matter of days before it completely took her over. Janice had not eaten in over a week and was gaunt and tired. Not long from the beginning of their fight, Janice gave up with a whimper, "Who the hell are you? Leave me alone...."

"Janice, I am Love. I know you remember me, sweetheart. I know you do. It will take some time and this will all make sense. I have something for you to see and it will be hard to look at."

"No!"

"Janice, I need you to do this for me. You will not like it. But it will not hurt you. I'm only trying to help."

Janice fought back as best she could but by now Amy was able to hold her arms together and down using only one hand. With the other, she reached deep in her pocket and retrieved a mirror. She flung it open in Janice's face and said, "Look Janice. This is what it has done to you."

Janice looked in horror at her face. She was weak and her skin hung low from her high cheekbones. Her face was ashen grey like the sky outside and her eyes dark, almost as black as night. Janice reeled back from the image in the mirror. "No!!!"

The house revolted immediately. The wailing of a hundred voices blasted through every crevice of the walls and sunk themselves deep into the ears of everyone present. It shrieked at them both and pleaded with Janice to remain inside it.

"Janice this isn't you! I know you are a beautiful lady! I am going to help you, Janice! Just trust me. The Shadow is doing this to you!"

"Get me out of here!" Janice screamed.

Amy knew that was all it took. She wanted Janice to have the desire to leave however short lived it may be. Amy scooped her up and ran back to the top of the ladder as the looming, breathing walls screamed in anger. A large beam from above swung down hard toward her head and Amy jumped with Janice in her arms through the man-made hole in the floor, bypassing the ladder completely and landing hard on the second floor. As she landed, the beam crashed hard on the floor above them. Amy knew she had to be quick.

She put Janice down and grabbed her hand, pulling it over her shoulders and kneeling down so that Janice could climb on her back. Nails from the floor that had been there a hundred years began popping and flying upward, sinking into the ceiling above.

One of them tore through Amy's skin on her left calf and she winced in pain, trying hard not to scream. The Shadow reacts to everything. It would react to her scream and zero in on punishing her in that moment. It is relentless and Amy knows it.

"Amy!" She could hear Farron from inside the house, downstairs on the first floor. He sounded wild with rage and fear. He had come only to save her. Amy wished he had only done what he was told. But this was also a sign that he had what it may take be Jack's Hero.

"Get out, Farron!" Amy exclaimed as she darted down the stairs. The old wooden door at the bottom swung open and closed rapidly slamming itself as if to break itself into pieces. The walls breathed heavily and labored now. They screamed long and loud at her to get out and begged Janice to stay just a moment longer.

Just a moment, Janice and we will be great! Just one more second Janice! Janice you owe me one second after everything I have given you!

Amy held Janice to her back as hard as she could and dove hard to the bottom of the stair case and through the slamming door, rolling across the wood floor at the bottom level. It had calmed down some here. The Shadow was still upstairs where Janice had been for so long. Amy set her down and walked outside arm in arm with her.

****

Farron was waiting in the foyer arms open to help, eyes wide and skin white. He was terrified.

"Amy, what in the hell was all of that? Let go of her! You don't know if she's sick, Amy!"

"Oh she is sick. But I can't catch it and neither can you if you keep your head in the game here, Farron."

Farron lent a hand to Amy by reaching under Janice's left arm to help her out of the house. Janice immediately jerked back away from him and spat at him. "Stay away from me, redneck!" she growled.

Farron reeled back hurt and in disbelief at the rude remark. "She's still not herself, Farron. She's really confused right now. Let's get her something to eat and take it easy for a bit. With the right people around her, she'll come back. She's not too far gone."

"Well I'd sure as hell like to see what "too far gone" is. Better yet, I'd like not to see it." He said. Amy hung her head.

"You may get to see it, Farron." She replied. This is only the tip of a very ugly iceberg if Jack's as bad as I think he is.

Eli waited for them outside and when he saw Janice, he fell to his knees. He felt immediately guilty for not having gone in to get her months ago. He laid the weight on his shoulders and cried uncontrollably. Janice looked at him and sneered his way.

Truthfully, Eli had been in such a cloud of confusion and despair that there would have been no way that he could've gotten her out anyway. He knew this. But it was difficult for him to see someone that he loved and cared for so much in this shape, especially knowing that he was only a few hundred yards away at any time.

Amy looked at him and said, "Eli it took a lot to get her out of there. You could have never done it yourself."

"But..."

"But nothing! It isn't your fault and to blame yourself right now isn't going to help at all. I need you to be here and as alert as possible."

"I don't see how that is possible," he replied.

"Eli, we are all going to sit down and talk about this and come up with a plan to get Jack. That is why Farron and I are here. But I need as few Shadows to contend with as possible. We all have to stay together and you will be an active part of putting this land back together."

"What's the chances of us failing?"

"It doesn't matter, Eli. If we don't do anything, we're dead anyway."

"That's one way to look at it."

"No, Eli. That's the way it is."

CHAPTER SEVENTEEN

"Eli, do you have any other place than that house for us to eat something and get cleaned up?"

"Yeah that building above the bunkhouse is an outdoor kitchen and shower house."

"Great. That'll work."

With Janice still latched on to Amy's arm and looking wildly about, they all headed up the hill. When they arrived, Farron held the door for Amy and Janice. Eli followed them inside and Farron closed the door behind them. Amy lay Janice down on a couch next to the door and sat below her on the floor. Janice just lay there staring upward and through the boundaries of the room somewhere else that neither of them knew where at that moment. "Janice, don't listen to it. It is lying to you. You have to try and stay with me." Janice didn't acknowledge her words at all.

"Eli, what do you have to eat?"

"Probably not much; but I'll check."

"Farron, go with him, please."

"You got it, boss." he replied

Farron followed Eli into the dark kitchen and pulled the lighter from his overall pocket to light a candle that sat on the outdoor kitchen's dining table. It was nothing fancy, just an old rickety table that Eli had picked up at a yard sale somewhere back in town. But it fit the room. Everything was used or recycled from some previous life in a family's home somewhere. The candle-light revealed some books on shelves that were built into the walls around him, an old electric stove and oven next to an unkempt sink full of dishes just like the main house. To his right, was a wall of large windows that looked back down toward the bunkhouse. The floor was poured concrete just like the little front room. A door led further back to three showers and a toilet. The whole building itself was walled with pine boards and a had a sheetrock ceiling that Eli and Jack, and several others, had labored on for weeks to have it all done before winter a few years prior.

Those were better days, back then. They were full of fun and laughter. Summer days were full of long hours working on projects like this. But they gave way to cooler evenings with iced tea and big dinners everyone cooked for one another. The garden was a full time job and produced big heirloom vegetables and raspberries. Janice loved to can the raspberries and make jams and everyone spread it on their toast. What a treat it was those lovely summers they spent together like a family. The winters were spent indoors at the big table playing Hearts by the heat of a little wood stove. The little time they spent outside was used to cut wood and to play in the snow when it fell, pulling one another around on an old car hood flipped upside down and heinously transformed into a sled.

But those days seemed so far away, now. They only cried a distant cry of loneliness from the back of the minds of the people that lived it. Everyone was lost and scared and apart from that part of themselves. It seemed unattainable. It seemed as if only a childhood memory that you can't quite remember all the details. You just remember that is was so good while it lasted.

"Cracker's, Farron. That's all I've got is damn crackers!"

"Well, that'll have to do," Farron replied.

He took a box of the crackers from Eli and brought them into the front room. Janice was sitting up on the couch now. But she still appeared to stare blankly at the floor, showing now emotion whatsoever. Amy took the crackers and as Farron began to sit next to her, she told him to leave her with Janice and sit with Eli. He understood and walked back into the kitchen. Eli sat at the table, head in his hands just as Jack had found him months earlier. Farron walked over to the table and pulled up a chair to sit down with him.

"When's the last time you ate, buddy?"

"I don't know. I'm not hungry."

"Listen, Eli. I am not the 'know it all' here. Hell, I barely know what is going on. She picked me up drunk on the side of the road just a few days ago. But, I do know that whatever we're dealing with here is pretty big and you should probably suck it up and eat something."

Eli stared at him angrily for his frank statement. But soon after, it melted to defeat and he reached down in the box and began to nibble the edge of a cracker, and then another. It didn't take long to recognize how hungry he was and all politeness left. He devoured half the box in no time.

"You wanna know what we're dealing with here, buddy?"

"Jesus Christ man, tell me! The wonderful witch of the west talks in circles and I can't make heads or tails of what she is saying!"

"I heard that Farron! I am not a damn witch! I am love!" Amy chimed in from the next room.

"You see what I mean?" Farron replied to Eli.

"Farron she really is love. We all have a Hero of some sort inside us. Some recognize theirs more than others. Some feed theirs more than others. Amy happens to have fed hers very well. You have one as well, buddy. You just have yet to realize it. Amy sees it in you though, or you would not be here. I knew she was familiar to me. I have met her many times throughout my life. She, of course never came to me as Amy. But she has always appeared as love."

"So basically what you're saying is that she really is the wonderful witch of the west?"

"Amy is just Amy. But Amy, as well as only a few others on this planet is able to embody love to the extent of some of our greatest spiritual leaders. Amy has channeled loved so thoroughly that she can make things happen that are much bigger than most can understand. The "Super-Natural" happens all around you, Farron, all of the time. We are just usually blind to it or we find a way to explain it to make sense within the world in which we live. Adversely, Jack is consumed with another entity that we all have because we have all created our own. He is overtaken by his Shadow. That is the term we use, Farron. Yours was the reason you drank the way you did. You aren't a bad person. But when your Shadow took hold of you, for whatever reason it did, you turned hard to the bottle and remained in a stupor, not just when you were drunk. But it consumed you to drink more, find more, worry about running out and so on and so on."

"I see."

"You almost do. See Farron you have a Hero as well. Like I said before, we all do. I am only assuming that your Hero is a great protector. I get that sense from you. Jack's Hero was a great protector as well. It was loyal and full of love for other people."

"What do you mean it 'was' that way?" said Farron.

"Jack murdered his Hero."

"What? How do you...?" Farron shook his head trying to take all of this information in. "So, where is this young man right now?"

"Jack stays down at the river in the mouth of a cave. I have only been down there a few times; you know when he wasn't so bad."

"No, Eli. I don't know."

"He is completely consumed now. I don't really know that this is going to work. But, Amy insists that we try and that if we don't try the outcome will be horrible."

Farron asked, "So, where do you think I fit in this whole crazy equation?"

"That's probably for Amy to say Farron. I don't know. But you will know when the time is right." Farron stared at Eli across the candlelit table and tried to read his face. Farron knew that Eli could probably tell him exactly why he was here. He just wasn't going to and Farron knew there was no way to make him. So, he slumped back in his chair and took a deep breath.

"You got any beer?"

"No, Farron. I don't drink and you shouldn't right now either. You never know. . ."

"Eli!" Farron interrupted. "I was making a joke."

For the first time in almost a year, a smile cracked Eli's lips and he was careful to retrieve it before it got too far away from him.

Amy had convinced Janice to take a few bites of a cracker only twenty minutes prior to the entire box being empty. She still was not herself. However, she had at least eaten, which was a feat in and of itself. Janice was now sitting up and looking around the room instead of staring through the walls. Amy tried to engage her in a little conversation, nothing too heavy. Janice gave simple yes or no answers or she refrained from speaking at all. Amy figured she was probably very confused and not sure which reality was real. Amy tried to imagine what must be going through her mind.

"W-Why did you c-c-come here?" stuttered Janice.

It was the first time she had volunteered a question since kicking her in the head so Amy was thrilled. A smile came across Amy's pretty face and Janice turned her head quickly to not have to see her happiness. Shame was all she knew and the thought of a smile was certainly stomach turning to Janice in the shape she was in. Amy recognized her retreat from the conversation and composed a blank mask of apathy to help Janice feel more comfortable. After a few seconds, Janice looked back and posed the question again now that Amy had lost the smile.

"Janice, I am here to help, as I have said before. I will explain more as you get to feeling better. I am going to need your help on a few things then. But for now, I guess you could say that Jack sort of inadvertently invited me to help out with your situation.

"J-J-Jack hasn't done much good for this place. I c-c-can't imagine him inviting you was a good idea either."

"Eli said you might be hard to convince."

"I will be."

"Well for now, why don't get some sleep and let's talk about this tomorrow."

"Will it come for me here?"

"Yes, it probably will come in your sleep, Janice. But I am here and will wake you and bring you back. You aren't too far gone."

"Jack is though, huh?"

"Go to sleep Janice. I will be right here."

"I could leave if I wanted."

"No, I won't let you, Janice. Not tonight."

Janice was exhausted. There was no doubting that. She didn't like this young girl telling her what to do. But, she was simply too tired to put up more than just a little resistance. The weight of the Shadow had been lifted from her for now. It felt so good to be away from it. But the Shadow was just a heavy blanket. It wouldn't take long for her to trade its weight for its security. She remembered clearly having her own strength and not relying on the Shadow for her power. She gained that personal strength from something that she hadn't experienced in quite some time. It seemed a memory faded by time to her. *What had that thing been? From where did I get the power? Why do I not have it? It's my power! It belongs to no one else but me! Where did it go?*

Her eyes became heavy with the thoughts that crowded her mind. It was too much to think about tonight. She finally took Amy's advice and laid down on her right side in order to not have her back to anyone or anything. She closed her eyes and let out a sigh. It was only a minute or so later that she slept peacefully.

Amy got up and grabbed a blanket from the other side of the room and walked over to this lady that seemed to despise her presence. Despite the one way disgust, Amy covered her up and blew the candle out next to her. It was early still. The sun was just going down. But Amy figured if she could keep the Shadow at bay, Janice would easily sleep all night and the more good sleep she got the better things would go tomorrow and the quicker they could all get to Jack. Amy barred the front door from the inside with a wooden board and placed several pieces of silverware from the kitchen on top of it. That way, if anyone moved through the only way out, she would hear it. She turned and waked into the kitchen where Eli and Farron still sat talking.

"How's she doing?" asked Eli.

"Well, she is talking and ate a box of crackers. She told me what a dummy I was and now she is asleep."

"Well at least she spoke her mind, sis,"

"Very funny, Farron."

"Eli, how are you feeling?" Amy asked

"I am feeling like my land is over-run with lunatics and I am out of hardly anything to eat."

"Tomorrow I'll go into town and pick up a few things, if you want," proposed Farron.

"Sure. You take Eli with you and I will stay here and work with Janice until you get back. In fact, why don't you go in the morning, as soon as you get up?"

"Done deal, Sis."

The candlelight was all that flickered in the room. It bounced off of everyone's face. It darted its amber glow in and out of every corner of the small room. The only sound was the occasional crackle of the wick and the wind still blowing against the windows outside. No one knew what to say. There was nothing to say. They just sat there in silence until Amy finally spokaye up and said, "This is good. We need to be comfortable together in silence."

"Amy what kind of plan do you have? Give it up," said Eli.

"Well, the first thing is that we all need to be comfortable with one another. We need to understand one another to the extent that we read each other without so much speaking. Eli, do you feel up to a lodge tomorrow?"

"I don't know. That takes a lot of energy and time."

"I understand Eli. I at least want you to build a fire. The fire will only be extinguished by us when we have Jack or by nature when we are all dead. Other than that, it must continue to burn as a symbol of our mission and purpose. It will keep us grounded and everyone will be responsible for it."

"We aren't damn Indians, Sis."

"I am more than aware of that Farron. However, it is the best ceremony for togetherness and purpose and yet it still retains an introspective quality, as well." Farron looked at her confused. "You're going to have to trust me on some of this." She said

"Well, I'm tired as hell. I am going to lie down and get some sleep." Said Farron

"It's going to be a long night tonight, Farron. You're going to have to sleep in the chair you're sitting in just in case I need you. I am going to rest my back against the front door and stay there. Farron, no one leaves these two rooms without someone else knowing. Got it?"

"Well, if you say so."

Farron laid his big head and shoulders down on the table like a child that had been scolded in school and Eli leaned back in his chair as far as he could. Amy left the candle burning for the time being and stepped back in to check on Janice. She was still sleeping peacefully. It would only be twice that night that Amy would have to wake up and calm her down, bringing her back to reality and driving the Shadow back. She felt it come through the door both times and was awake by the time it hit Janice.

For Amy, the morning couldn't come quickly enough.

CHAPTER EIGHTEEN

As the sun labored hard to crest the blank horizon, the clouds continued to choke it back, but not quite as hard as they did the day before. For a moment, the sky was turning its old familiar brilliant red in the east. But soon, the blackened clouds that loomed overhead would choke the sunlight back to a silver sickness that permeated the mood of any living thing it reached. Amy lay with her back still against the door and noticed a blue opening all around the visible horizon. She did not know if the clouds had grown or shrunk. *Was the blue visible yesterday?* She tried hard to remember and was sure that it was not. She didn't have the luxury of watching the sunset and comparing it to its rise because she had locked herself in this building and was focused on everyone else as the sun had been waning into the black night.

Her back ached and her butt was numb from the cold concrete floor and the pressure that drove the blood out, leaving the familiar tingle. She had to get up and move. She felt jarred in this miserable sitting position. With a twist of her head, she could only seem to roll herself over, knees and hands on the floor and pull herself up slowly by grasping the oversized pine doorframe. Amy swore she could hear her bones cracking as she pushed and pulled herself upward. But they did not. Now standing, Amy looked back at the couch. Janice was not on it. She became frantic and impulsively switched her head to eye the door. It was closed. *Hell, it had to be closed! I was just lying against it!* In three large swift bounds, Amy burst through the little door into the next room, breathing heavy and shouting inexplicable phrases in her frantic frustration.

"Hey You! What the! Where!"

Janice swung around fast from the sink in the little room with a shocked look upon her face and let out a scream that she cut short upon realizing it was Amy. Upon hearing Janice Scream, Farron jerked upward off the table and fell backward in his chair with a crash to the floor yelling an obscenity. Eli jumped forward knocking the candle over. As it slid across the table, the flame extinguished quickly. The hot wax poured out and dripped slowly down Farron's open and upturned overall leg. Everyone stood completely still staring, shocked at one another.

"Yeeeowwww!"

Farron screamed at the top of his lungs and somehow inhumanly lunged forward from his lying position directly back into the table crunching the already broken glass of the candle under his boots.

"What the hell, Amy!" he yelled.

More silence. They all stood in silence, saying nothing. What could they say? Eli was frozen, lying halfway across the table, uncomfortable, but terrified to move an inch. Amy and Janice stood, mouths open and eyes wide staring blankly at one another. Poor Farron , in unbelievable pain, hands in the air and overalls peeled over his large frame and laying around his feet, with red wax splotched all over his leg and inner right thigh. They were a sight to see and upon realizing their predicament, Amy laughed, doubled over. She couldn't quit laughing. Eli continued his Superman like position over the table for a moment, only slowly returning to his chair. Janice continued to look confused and Farron was frozen in near nude desperation, only an ounce away from pure shame.

"You know, Sis, that's really not that funny." He said, reaching to pull up his overalls.

"You're right, Farron! This is absolutely hilarious!"

"How you 'spect this bunch of fools to get anywhere on your space mission?" he exclaimed.

His statement just drove her further into mad laughter and she had to sit down and take a breath. Amy took a chair between Eli and Farron.

"Oh, Whew! Oh my God! We are definitely a bunch to look at here. But this is no space mission Farron. You're going to have to get your head in the game."

"Well, Guru Joe, pouring hot wax on my testiculars is getting my head in nothing but a quick way outa here, Sis!"

"Calm down, Farron." Amy pleaded.

Janice made her way to the table, shifting her eyes to the right and left. She seemed to be waiting for another catastrophe and determined to not let it surprise her this time. Eli rubbed his eyes and attempted to sit as straight as possible in his chair. Farron buttoned his overalls back on and sat down slowly, grimacing at the pain in his right leg.

"Hell of a wake-up call, Eli!"

"Farron! Shut up! He didn't mean to!"

Farron grumbled under his breath. Amy gathered the attention of everyone at the table and first inquired as to how Janice was feeling. She still did not speak a word. But she nodded to Amy in some sort of agreement that she seemed to be alright. Amy decided to take what she could get and not push her too hard. She knew Janice would come around sooner or later. Furthermore, she took Janice for a sort of introvert. She imagined that Janice, even at her best, enjoyed the solitude of peaceful self and while she may have many that she loves, she knows them much better than they do her. She was a wonderful friend to have. But, she kept you at an arm's length for the purpose of easy evaluation in case she needed to protect herself. Some had read her wrong in the past. But Janice was a wonderful woman; she just loved her personal integrity and the integrity of her sacred space and she protected it as a warrior protects his family.

"Alright then, Eli and Farron will you go get some food from town while I sit here and work with Janice?"

Eli spoke up, "Of course. Are you ready to leave Farron?"

"Mmmhmm" Farron replied still angry over the candle.

"None of the cars here have any gas" said Eli, ashamed that he had let them run out. Grief over his desperate situation had overtaken his duty to the land he loved.

"That's okay, Eli; just take my car and get some extra fuel while you're there."

Eli and Farron stepped out of the foyer of the outdoor kitchen and back to the seemingly cursed earth that supported them and everything they did. Farron first and then Eli, broke the threshold of the door and the grey light of the sun soaked their skin. It wasn't much as far as sunlight goes. But it was light, nonetheless. They made their way to Amy's little red Honda which was still parked at the top of the hill near the tree line that separated them from the forest within which Jack was still held. Their boots stomped hard against the dirt path as they ascended the grade. Once to the car, Farron stopped and pulled a cigarette from his bib pocket.

"Wanna smoke?"

"I don't smoke, Farron."

"Wasn't askin' if ya did. I's askin' if yeh wanted one."

Eli turned sharply to Farron. "Farron, what do you want to be in all of this?"

"What are you talkin' 'bout?

"Get in the car." said Eli.

Farron lowered his head and pushed his big right leg into the floorboard of the little red Honda. He squeezed the rest of himself behind the little wheel and sat as far back as possible, jerking and pushing back against the seat until it was situated to some relative comfort.

"Farron, you are going to have to decide at what level you wish to be involved in all of this. I mean, we need you and you are an important part of her plan. But, we don't need you to be half-way invested. Farron, are you prepared to give yourself to this purpose or are you just along for the ride?"

"I'm 'fraid there might be a wrong answer to that."

"Oh, there is Farron. But, the answer should not determine the outcome. So, just shoot it to me."

Farron's thick Ozark accent often arrived with a high tide of anxiousness, frustration, or sometimes humor. But during important dialect and a meaningful conversation, his words were chosen more carefully by him and spoken more clearly. It was not Farron's nature to speak in this way. However, he did want people to be able to understand him and respect his opinion. Eli's question seemed serious. Farron cleared his throat and began his response.

"Y' know Eli, I just don't quite get you people all the time. Are ya'll a cult? I am not sure about all this Hocus Pocus, Eli. It freaks me out and I do not know if I should believe and jump in this thing head first, or if I oughta run and take outa here like a jack rabbit."

"It would seem to me that your heart led you here in the first place."

"I was taking care of that girl," Farron grumbled.

"Oh yeah, Farron. So, you were taking care of her" Eli said with obvious doubt. "How well were you taking care of her while you were laying in the gutter, drunk?"

Farron just sat still, looking through the glass. He was embarrassed by the sarcastic remark. *What do I say to that? How could he say that to me? Well, she did help me. But I came out here to protect her! I know that's why!* Farron thought of every way out of the seeming defeat that was before him. Eli was waiting for an answer.

"I guess she has been taking care of me, Eli. Are you happy with that?" Farron said with further shame.

"How do you feel, right now, Farron?"

"I feel like a damn fool. I just admitted to you that I had to be taken care of by a little girl, Eli."

"That shame is the Shadow, Farron. The false pride that made you try and convince me that you were here to help Amy is the Shadow. The shame that led you to utilize your false pride is the Shadow, Farron. The Shadow is all of those things. Do you understand? Do you see how they control your life?"

"I see it. What I don't see is how that turns us into supernatural goblins that run around in the woods and turn weather patterns upside down."

"That's a fair question. It must seem awfully strange here to you, Farron. You see, some people give their lives to work. Some people give their lives to church or family. Some people give their lives to their possessions. Some of the most destructive people give their lives, only to themselves. But we gave our lives to something different, here. We gave our lives to the Universe. We gave our lives to infinite possibility and in turn we brought that possibility and every aspect of this universe to the land on which you stand. This is our proving ground. It is as real as you see and hear it. All of the possibilities exist because we have allowed them to. It may seem strange to you, only because you have never allowed for the possibility of anything more than whatever it is you drink over. That is the end-all of your experience. In fact though, you shouldn't feel too bad. You are among the majority."

Farron took his words to heart. But he still had questions. "Is it real or not real? It cannot be both ways, Eli. Right?"

"Farron, it is whatever you want it to be. It is whatever you create in your life."

The car rattled further down the old dirt road. They broke the line of trees and left the ranch behind for a moment and Eli felt a fear creep into him. The fear told him to return; to turn the car around and go back. He asked the fear, *to where should I go back and what do I do when I get there?* The fear replied to go back to his tree house and hide from all of this. *Get out!* He screamed, in his mind to the Shadow. *Get Out! You aren't welcome! You have a fight on your hands and we will win! Jack is his own man! He does not belong to you!*

The sun began to peek into the car and warm the dash as they barreled down the road and Eli knew the Shadow had stayed behind him. His affirmation had driven it back. He knew that fear could be a healthy caution to something that was potentially harmful. But more often than not, it was nothing more than the Shadow putting a halt to personal progress. All he had to do was ask the right question and wait for the wrong answer. The Shadow always gave the same answer and that answer was to never protect yourself from harm. It was always to tell him:

Because you aren't enough. You aren't worthy. You cannot succeed.

If the answer boiled down to that, the Shadow was at work and affirming its presence drove it away. The Shadow preferred to work in the darkness and only make itself known when the person was utterly dependent on it to survive. At that point, it didn't matter who knew of its presence. It didn't matter if it was wanted or not. By that point, it was needed.

****

Janice stood before Amy at the pit by the lodge and stared into her eyes. The clouds were overhead. The wind blew. But, the sound of the leaves rattling was not there at all. In fact, all outside sounds remained far from this space. This space was sacred and could not be entered by things such as distracting sounds. Love made sure this was a safe place and Janice was here only by Love's invitation.

"Is it there, Janice?"

"It is."

"Can you tell it to leave?"

"No."

"Can I tell it to leave?"

"I wouldn't do that."

"Janice, do not allow your fear to answer. I want you to answer."

"But…"

"No, I want you to answer. I do not need the Shadow's permission. I only need yours. Do I have your permission to ask it to leave?"

Janice's face twisted again with frustration and fear. Her pretty eyes welled with large salty tears. They pooled in her eyes until they ran over and trickled down her tired cheek. She let out a breath, swallowed hard and breathed in, holding her breath in for what seemed like a very long time. With her next outward breath she let the words escape with a whisper.

"Yes, you have my permission."

Love leaned forward and took Janice's hands. She extended her arms so that the two were standing across from one another and pushing against each other, elbows only slightly bent and full pressure traded at the palms of their hands. Janice squinted and grimaced at Love and Love shook with power, pushing back. It was silent and the force between them was strong, pulsing with power and earnest determination. The Shadow was strong and while Janice was not entirely dependent on it, it was set in well and Janice was not comfortable asking it to leave. Amy knew this would take intense focus.

"Get out of her! She doesn't need you!"

Janice began to hear Love's words. They were sweet memories of an awesome power she once contained.

"Get out! She doesn't want you! She is only afraid of what it will be without you and you know it, Shadow! Get out!"

The Shadow pushed against her. It could not fight Love and Janice's will together. It felt the shift. It witnessed Janice's eyes opening and knew she was listening. It heaved its rasping breath and spit at her. It struggled in its footing and pushed with all its might against her.

You weren't invited! She is mine and you know it! She isn't listening to you! Turn around and go! The Shadow bellowed back at her.

Love did not turn around and go. In fact, she couldn't. She pushed on and grew strength from her own perseverance. Their feet dug sharply into the dusty earth. Their legs burned in the muscles from straining to topple one another. Backs arched and elbows now locked, they screamed at one another and pushed until Janice finally lost her footing and fell backward to the ground. Amy stayed on top of her and pinned her down.

"Are you out? If not, you better get out! Janice you can tell it to leave! You are powerful enough without the Shadow! Tell it Janice! Tell it! Tell it to leave!"

"Get out of me!"

Janice's scream echoed across the valley. The sound returned to the space and Janice's eyes opened slowly and blinked a few times before she let her breath out once again.

"How do you feel, Janice?" said Amy

"Different... I feel different."

"Is it better?"

"Yes... Yes, it is. Thank you."

"There is nothing to thank me for, Janice. You did it. I just reminded you of the power you already had."

"No, I really want to thank you. You saved me."

"If you want to thank me, darling, help me make that fire we talked about earlier."

JEREMY NICHOLAS HERO

CHAPTER NINETEEN

The fire was burning hot, so hot that Janice and Amy had stepped away from it, still in the circle that the space for the lodge provided. But they were far enough away to keep from blistering their skin. Janice was exhausted. But she felt free of the Shadow for once and held an inner strength that she had only remembered as something sweet yet so far away only a few hours earlier. They had worked hard to gather the loose dying logs that lie on the ground and get the fire going. Amy felt strongly that their efforts would pay off. The effort was worth it. There seemed to be light at the end of this tunnel. She wondered if they would be strong enough to thwart Jack's Shadow and she could not say with utter confidence that they would be. But, she knew without a doubt that they were better off going in prepared.

She thought to herself, *my father would be proud.* He had given her so much. He had loved her like no other and she went to him in her thoughts because she knew his answers to her toughest questions would be fearless and full of love. He had taught her independence, her love for mankind and her drive for spreading that idea of self-sufficiency and love to everyone she met. He was here with her now. He was waiting for her like he had always been before. She knew she would have to see him someday. But until then, her path was constantly changing and her feet took her to people that needed her, no matter where they may be.

The familiar sound of gravel crunching under a set of tires filled their ears and Janice looked up to see the little red Honda traveling back down the long drive.

"It looks like they're back, Amy."

"It would appear so. Stay here with the fire and rest, please and I will go down to them."

Janice sat down and Amy began the short steep trek down to the parking place. Janice watched her walk away. She was a beautiful girl that seemed to float wherever she went, delicately traveling over the rock landscape without fail or fall. Many women, and men for that matter, had visited the ranch for many years. A lot of them had difficulty traversing the rocky ground and stumbled about like newborn calves learning their balance. But it was if Amy adapted immediately and had no issue whatsoever with it. In fact, it was as if she knew her way around. Janice liked her. She enjoyed her confidence and even though Janice rarely opened up to anyone, she felt in her heart that Amy was a safe soul in which to confide.

Farron stepped out of the car first as if to give Eli the room he needed to get himself out. He looked back once his large frame cleared the doorway and nodded in satisfaction as Eli lifted himself up and out of the little car.

"I think we got everything." Farron said.

"Great, guys! Now, let's bring it into the outdoor kitchen. That will have to be our base right now. It keeps us all together."

They began unloading groceries and supplies into the kitchen and Amy started to pilfer through it all to see if there was a way to make a meal out what they had brought back. It wasn't long before she was smiling; looking at what the two men she sent to the store had come back with. There was to be no fancy cooking which was probably all the better. Amy came up with a corn bread mix and several cans of kidney beans. It was simple. But it would be filling and could feed an army on a budget.

Farron stayed with her to help and Eli headed outside to sit beside the fire with Janice. She turned her head and looked at him briefly as he approached. His stride was long. He approached with caution as he had learned to do over the last year. She sat still, her eyes peering deep into the fire. Janice was as unsure of their conversation as was Eli. He knelt beside her and rested backward until he was in a comfortable sitting position. A time went by that they sat in silence and Eli then broke it.

"Janice, this was a beautiful place at one time wasn't it?"

"It was, Eli. But I told you not to let him come out here."

"I cannot turn him away, even now. You know that about me."

"Oh I do, Eli. You have sold this damn place to the wolves for as long as I can remember. Anybody that wants to come out here gets to and somehow you think they are all so great until they finally hurt you. This one has nearly destroyed you and you are going to go save him! I will never understand you!"

"Wrong, Janice. We are going to go save him."

"Why, Eli? What is there to save?"

"That is the Shadow talking, Janice. Were you worth saving?"

"I don't know."

Janice paused. She knew she was being hard to get along with. She wanted Eli to see that opening the doors to this place to just anyone was not helping the land. It was hurting it and them in her opinion. Eli could not see it that way. To exclude someone, was to be acting out of fear and he just wouldn't have it.

"Eli, that is what the problem has always been! You cannot open this place to people that would harm it."

"There has to be better way to put that, Janice. Even great people sometimes harm one another. We try not to. But to say, 'I will exclude anyone from my life that may cause me harm, does just that. It harms us. It keeps us secluded from opportunity!"

Just as they seemed to be getting nowhere; just as soon as Eli thought she was going to blow up at him in anger, she stopped. She leaned over and kissed his cheek and lay her head on his shoulder.

"I am scared. I know fear is talking to me Eli. I know it's the Shadow that tells me to exclude others from my life. But Eli, that is a part of me that I just don't think I want to let go of yet."

"Janice, I love you. But that will follow you until you can let it go. Listen, I believe you are correct in saying that we must strive to keep negative people and destructive forces away from this land. I believe you, Janice. I really do. However, I need you to understand that I cannot see the forest for the trees sometimes and you are typically staunchly against anyone getting to know you. We are like the two ends of a teeter totter and the pivot point is out there in the woods consumed by his Shadow. He protected this land, Janice and you know it."

Janice breathed deeply a sigh of agreement.

"I cannot argue that, Eli. But I still hold hope that we can do it alone."

"What? And leave him out there? The Shadow is destroying him and he will eventually destroy us Janice, unless we save him or kill him. You know that as well as I do. We cannot just leave him alone."

"I know, Eli. Listen, I am on board. I am not happy about it. But for whatever it is worth, I am on board."

"It's worth a lot because we need you. You are a protector. I am a lover."

Janice lifted her head and smiled at him. The corners of her mouth turned upward and revealed her grace and beauty. It was what he had fallen in love with so long ago, that gorgeous smile. His mind could hear her laughing the laugh that stole his heart. A familiar warmth filled Eli's heart with joy. But the joy was bittersweet. He could not have her now for himself. He could reach no further than she would allow. He wouldn't feel his body next to hers under a warm blanket. Too much damage was done and Eli had wandered this land away from her. She had moved on with herself and Eli had tried had to do the same with projects and missions of his own. They both still loved one another. There was no doubting that. Their love was just expressed with a glance or an occasional touch on the shoulder and that is where it stopped. It had stopped there long ago.

"Hey are ya'll hungry!"

Eli was starving. But he didn't want to move. He didn't want to get up and leave Janice or this moment. Farron plopped down beside him, oblivious to the moment.

"Hey, I asked if ya'll was hungry. I brought you two bowls of beans and cornbread. Here ya go. I'll go get mine and me and Amy will join ya."

Eli took Janice's bowl and passed it to her and rested his in his lap. Farron bounded back to the outdoor kitchen to retrieve Amy and their food.

"That was nice, Eli"

"Yes, yes it was." He said, surprised.

Only a moment later, Farron came back with Amy. They all sat in a circle around the fire that had died down enough to be a comfortable heat source rather than a scorching remnant of Hell. They didn't speak much as they were all ravenously hungry and devouring the hot beans and cornbread like it was their last meal.

After they finished the meal, everyone lay around by the fire and just enjoyed their full bellies and being able to relax for a moment. Janice broke the silence.

"Let's get to business, guys. When are we going to go after him and how?"

"Let's try and enjoy this night" said Amy. "Tomorrow, we will prepare to go and the next morning is when I plan on making the move down the river to get Jack."

"I'm still not sure what you want me to do, Sis."

"Farron, I need someone strong. You are that person. I need that protective spirit of yours. The rest of it, you will get later."

"So there will be a fight?" he replied.

"Farron, this will be a fight you will never forget. It will be as unreal as you dream of and as real as you can imagine. Prepare for anything."

JEREMY NICHOLAS HERO

CHAPTER TWENTY

The tall sycamore tree cracked under the pressure of its dead weight. It groaned sadly its scream of twisted dead fibers being ripped from one another. The sandy dirt that held it firmly in the ground gave way to its sheer weight and size and the dirt disintegrated as the dying roots of the tree sprung upward out of the ground. It began to tip and lean, unsure of its destination. It seemed to contemplate where it may want to fall, if only for a brief moment. Once it reached the tipping point, the point of no return, the tree gained momentum like a freight train out of control and the sound of it was like thunder in the canyon.

Jack heard the tree begin to fall and crawled like an animal on all fours with amazing strength and agility across the cave floor. He perched upon the rim of the cave and thrust his head out of the gaping mouth. Twisting his head back and forth, he finally gained his bearings just in time to watch it fall directly across the cave's opening. Jack dodged the huge white trunk and in the same split second in his delirium, jumped from the rocky ledge onto the falling mammoth and attacked it as it crashed to the dark forest floor. The limbs bent backward with the great force of the free-fall and whipped his naked back as he pulled and scratched at the smaller limbs. As the tree was only feet from crashing to the ground, Jack braced himself hard against the trunk. Then just in time, he let go and leapt upward to save himself the terrible blow. As he came back down, he landed perfectly upon the trunk, crouched and snarling with hatred. His lower jaw dislocated and he buried his head low and sunk his teeth into the old sycamore as deep as he could.

Jack was an animal. Completely possessed by the Shadow, his strength had grown immensely and his hatred for anything that threatened his power, abounded over any other emotion. In fact, all emotion had been obliterated from existence for Jack and he did not even know his name. He did not know himself as Jack anymore. He only knew himself as the servant of his own fears. He was his Shadow's puppet and survived only at the expense of what existed freely beside him. Nothing was immune from his attack. If it got in his way, it died, simple as that.

His body was bent over. He rarely stood upright and had reformed his total existence to surviving in the cave. He wore only what was left of his clothing. His shirt had been long gone and his bare feet had calloused well. He could traverse the forest floor like any other animal he encountered. What was left of his pants was still attached to him. But they were ripped to shreds. His back and arms were stronger than they had ever been. But they bore deep scars and bruises, as did the rest of his body. These were clearly visible. His hair was a matted mess and his stench filled the river bottom for a quarter mile in any direction. The sunlight beaming in little silver slivers from atop the bluff was a burning nuisance and he knew that whatever was up there was intent on ending him. He wanted to scale up the bluff and run through the forest toward them, killing them one by one. He had practiced in the cave and on the riverbank in the dark. He had practiced breaking their necks and tearing their throats out with his teeth. To end them meant it became his forest and his alone. He could then come up off the river bank and feast upon the fresh ground, driving the sunlight back as far as possible. He knew that whatever sunlight they brought with them would weaken him to the point of possibly being defeated. So, he dared not go up there until the Shadow said it was safe.

He did nothing without the Shadow's approval. It allowed him to hunt and get stronger. It allowed him to hone his killing skill. But it did not allow wonderment and questions. He knew not to ask questions. The Shadow was good to him and let him eat. It let him kill and spill blood on the riverbank. It sent him dreams, dreams of carnivorous ecstasy and sexual ecstasy. Although a woman's body still entered his thoughts, he knew that part of him was distant and dead. The Shadow kept him satisfied in his sleep. So, there was no use for a real woman. Those things were gone in the distance. They were not needed anymore. Not even a hot meal or his beloved coffee meant anything to him. Cold fresh meat was what he subsisted on and he relished the taste of the blood his tongue squeezed from it as it kicked its last futile attempts at life. Jack destroyed everything and licked up the blood of its existence with haste and hatred.

****

From the top of the bluff, back at the ranch, everyone heard the tree crash and looked at one another as it did. Immediately afterward, they heard the shrill scream of an animal they had never heard.

"Was that a bobcat?" asked Farron.

Silence abounded among the four of them. A cold reality set in that it could not be an animal. It seemed that the shrill scream almost contained words; but, only almost. It was the sound of something that was surely wild. But it was a human's vocal chords that made this sound. An animal's scream is innately apathetic to most human ears. We, without studying the animal, could never know whether it was happy or scared or angry. We just know that it made a sound. This was an angry voice, a terrible scream filled with the hostility of a desperate need for terror.

After a few moments of awkward silence, Eli asked, "It's him isn't it?"

"Yes." replied Amy. "That is Jack."

"There is no way. It sounded horrible", said Janice.

Amy tried to dispel the anxiety with some sort of explanation and hope. "Jack is no longer Jack and it will take time get him back."

"What are the odds that we don't?" asked Farron.

"Don't what?"

"That thing, if it is Jack, sounds like it could kill every damn one of us. I wanna know what the odds are of us not saving him."

"He could, Farron. He could kill us, every one, if we make a mistake and if you are going to back away from this, now is the time to do it."

"Look Sis, I'm not backing away. I just like to know what my odds are like when I'm dealing with a goddamn Wildman in the woods. My chances aren't great. Alright. That's all I needed to know."

He trembled inside with the fear that anybody would have and everyone else did as well. They all knew that success was slim. But the mission was evident to all of them and, they had come this far; there was no turning back in anyone's mind. Amy recognized this as a fact in her mind as the sun crested the horizon on their last day before going down to save Jack, she knew it was time to share her plan with each of them.

The fire still burned and Eli had covered the sweat lodge with old canvas. It took several sheets of the tattered material to cover the entire branch structure. He had piled the stones they were to use in a large pile outside the circle to be brought in a few hours before. He stood like a statue, pitchfork in hand beside the fire, letting its heat scorch his sweating skin. It burned his flesh fiercely. But Eli remained in a meditative place in his mind that kept him firm on his feet. He tested himself, which he often told others not to do. Eli told other people this because he did not want the lodge to become a proving ground for egotistical people that would end up hurting themselves or someone else. But it is, in the purest sense of the term, a proving ground. There must be a certain amount of perseverance in the human spirit and Eli knew this was going to possibly be one of his greatest challenges. Therefore, he pushed his body to accept the heat of the fire and transcend that pain to power and personal strength. He did not boast it though. He accepted it with humility and his pride was that he was to be available for his lost brother.

Janice and Amy worked hard to create a meal that would prepare them for and sustain them in the woods. They made up baggies of jerky and a granola type mix that was easily transportable and would not spoil if they were out for any extended period of time. They prepared the beans and cornbread again for tonight because it seemed to really stick to the ribs and last, not leaving them hungry in only a few short hours.

Farron worked hard at gathering water in several large white containers they would carry with them to the river.

"Farron, could you begin gathering everything you can think of as a defensive weapon?" Amy asked him.

"A gun would be a great start" he replied.

"The goal here Farron, is obviously to not kill Jack unless our lives are in serious danger. So there will be no guns, no bow and arrow. I only want defensive things, ways to stop Jack, to injure him and to hold him down if captured."

Farron grabbed several of the canvas tarps not being used in the lodge. He sharpened sticks and gathered about fifty feet of rope, throwing it all into the bed of Eli's white pickup truck.

****

The Shadow remained in its place. It remained fed and satisfied. Deep inside the cave, beyond the mouth, its large room in which Jack lived was the Shadow's realm. The cave's large front room narrowed into a tiny hole in which Jack knew never to crawl until the Shadow beckoned him. The narrow hole had water running inside it. Jack slept to the sound of the water each night. It never stopped running. It flowed with the power that the Shadow provided Jack so graciously.

Inside the narrow watery hole, the path remained small and snaked backward deep inside the bowels of this cave called home. Only about seventy-five yards back into the watery tunnel, it opened. But when it did, it opened in a big way. The room was in the shape of a large conch shell. About one hundred feet to the top, it gained size toward the bottom and if lit up, one could see the swirling conch shell shape as it rose higher and higher, smaller and smaller until they came to the point at the top only about fifty to a hundred feet from the surface of the Earth.

The Shadow perched its black shiny body upon a ledge of the swirling conch shell and dripped drool to the bottom of the cavern. It pooled and swirled, flowing outward down the path that led back to Jack, falling over the mouth of the cave and splashing down to the river below. Its breath was a sulfur stench that would've made anyone's eyes water. Poison leaked from the pores in its skin that were wide enough to sink a fist into. The Shadow sat as still as a rabbit in the brush, hiding from the hunter. But it was large. It had grown big and strong from all of Jack's fruitful labor. It never moved except to take the occasional breath and then sink back into its stillness, continually dripping the saliva from its ugly lower jaw that extended out further than any other part of it. Its talon-like fingers grasped two adjacent ledges in the conch shell cave and its feet stood firm with the heavy weight of a thousand worries pressing down on the stalagmite on which it perched.

It stayed inside Jack's mind, speaking to him and giving orders. It was fed by the following of those directives. It always wanted more. The Shadow knew Jack's miserable existence would be shortened by it. It did not care. There would be more parasites to host. There would be more. There was always another standing by for it to sink its claws into and drag down to their own demise. Its eyes flashed open, white and coated in a film with no pupil and no iris. It heard something from the top.

Footsteps… one person. They are moving slowly. Jack, someone is above us!

Jack heard the squeal of the Shadow and pounced up from the tree. "What is it, Shadow?"

It is only one person. They are moving slowly. It is probably a hunter.

"I will find them, Shadow. I will find them and bring them to you."

Jack, this will be a great test for you. Remember, if he is a hunter he will have a gun.

The hair on Jack's neck stood tall with excitement and he spun from the tree and made his way to the base of the bluff. He tried hard to hear the hunter at the top and could not. The Shadow's hearing was extraordinary. From inside the cave, every sound all around him crept inside and echoed over and over, giving him a three hundred and sixty degree radius to listen from. The saliva that ran out on the ground, out of the cave and to the river provided him the taste of anything passing by. These senses were used to warn Jack of any trouble and more importantly as an alarm if Jack ever strayed too far from the Shadow, itself.

Jack pounced onto the limestone face of the bluff and scaled upward as fast and as quietly as he could. Practicing this had paid off in a big way and Jack could be from the bottom of the three hundred foot bluff to the top within less than one minute. It was astounding how he moved now. The Shadow often reminded Jack that it was he who gave him this ability. Jack needed him and the Shadow knew it as much as Jack did himself.

Once at the bluff's crest, Jack held on to a tiny crevice and held his breath, listening for any sound that may be the hunter's footsteps or breathing. He waited and he waited until he finally heard a twig on the ground crack. The muscles in his arms flexed, getting ready to pull himself over the top to stand on the forest floor and attack his prey. A little while longer and the footsteps made themselves audible again. It was now a steady slow crunch in the leaves of years gone by. They have to be the cautious slow steps of a hunter. Steady... Steady...

Jack now you may go after him.

Jack lurched over the ledge of the bluff backward and rolled to a crouched position with no more sound that the rustling of a few leaves. It never crossed the hunter's ears, though. His footsteps continued slow and steady. Jack stood upright and faced several large boulders that climbed a shallow slope. The hunter would be on the other side. Jack's fists clenched upon themselves with anger and resentment toward the hunter for being in this place, his place, his land.

He placed a strong right hand on the first boulder and began inching his way across them and up the slope, careful to be quiet, but with enough speed so as to not let the hunter pass by him and be out of reach. He was still bound by the Shadow to never be too far away. The Shadow would certainly be angry and punish him if he did so.

By the time he reached the summit of the boulder field, he was peering down to where the hunter would pass, not making a single movement. Then he came into view. He was a middle aged man with shoulder length blonde hair, wearing anything but what Jack thought a hunter should wear. He had on khaki draw string cloth pants and he was not wearing a shirt. He carried a back pack instead of a gun over his naked white shoulder and although he did walk slowly and quietly. His walk was deliberate as if he meant to be there and intended on going somewhere. *What is this?* Thought Jack.

Kill the hunter, Jack!

"It isn't a hunter, Shadow."

I don't care what he is! Kill him! This is your chance. You know they will be coming for you, Jack; to take you away from me, to take your strength and all of the power I gave you! I said kill him!

Jack leapt from the last boulder and ran through the forest like a cheetah, his feet barely touching the leaves, his lungs barely exuding an ounce of air. With ease he traversed the forest floor, careful to stay behind the trees just in case the man saw him.

Within a few seconds he was within a stone's throw and the man turned to him. Jack expected him to scream and planned to latch down hard on his throat. But the man did not scream. He calmly extended his arm and lowered his head, keeping his eyes fixed on Jacks fast approach. From the backpack, he pulled a nice piece of hickory and when Jack leapt upward to ounce upon his prey. The man swung the hickory hard against him sending him directly to the ground. Jack lay there for only a moment and then arched his back and bounced to his feet. He looked bewildered at the man and then changed his face to stern, letting out a roar at the man with the backpack.

The man stood strong and proud. The wind whipped his hair about his face and shoulders. The man did not even blink. With the coldest icy blue eyes Jack had seen in a man, he just stared intently back at him. Bent at the knee, just slightly and his shoulder turned and hunched forward. The man appeared to be willing to pounce at any moment. Jack was certain that this was a formidable foe. But he would not back down without the Shadow telling him to do so. I cannot let Shadow down. I will not back down, regardless the outcome. Jack got ready to pounce at him again when the man spoke up.

"Jack, I am Charlie. You do not scare me. Retreat now and go back to your cave or I will kill you where you stand."

Jack snarled back at him.

Did he say, 'Charlie'?... Jack, did he say Charlie?

"Yes. Shadow he did."

Come back to me, boy. I need you here. Forget him.

"But Shadow, I..."

I said come back! Roared the Shadow.

Jack wrestled with the idea. He wanted the challenge. He wanted to make Shadow proud. But he knew if he didn't win, it would all be lost. The Shadow would leave him forever or he would be killed.

"Jack, the other option is to come with me. I will take you back to Eli. We can get you better. Would you like that?" Charlie said softly, as if he wanted to whisper to him.

Do not speak to him, Jack! He is lying! Come back here now!

The Shadow's saliva poured from the mouth of the cave now, gushing out. The cave trembled with his anger and the ground above quaked as if it felt the fear of the Shadow's presence. The Shadow breathed heavily. Its large pores steamed with the sulfuric stench.

Jack turned away and walked back to toward the edge of the bluff.

"I am serious Jack. I can take you back to the life you used to love. I know you won't do it. But I came to offer it to you." Charlie now spoke loudly in an attempt to get his attention.

Jack never turned around. As he approached the edge of the bluff, he only stopped for a brief moment to contemplate what was going on. But, he soon scaled back down it and crept back into the cave.

Good job, boy. You did the right thing.

"Why not him?" asked Jack aloud.

That is a battle you dare not fight, Jack. That is a battle for me and me alone.

"So, why doesn't he come after you?"

For us to fight, would not only destroy our home. It would destroy his as well.

CHAPTER TWENTY-ONE

As the lodge fire burned, everyone stood around it in silence. The rocks had been placed inside the fire about three hours ago and what was left of the sun crept away over the horizon. The fire burned hot and warmed the skin of everyone around. Its sparks lifted high up in the air like spirits bringing messages upward to the ether only to fall back to Earth as a white chalky dust once their work was complete. The night made no sound around them except the torturous breeze that never ceased. They lived in a world strongly affected by the Shadow. Although their positive influence had let the sun shine a little, they were only surviving in a broken remnant of what the land use to be. It would take hard work to bring the land back to its original state even if this battle was to be won.

Eli stood still with his pitchfork in hand and the wing of a hawk grasped in the other. Janice stood still, head bowed and prying in her own way for Jack, for Eli and everyone else involved. Farron stood in the circle, not fully understanding what was going on. But he was determined to ride this out to whatever end it may bring. Amy was the only one sitting and she held her arms outward as if waiting to catch something, some answer that may solve this problem of Jack and his Shadow in a more peaceful way. But there was none.

Just as Eli was about to announce that the rocks were ready, a voice came from the tree line that separated them from Jack and the Shadow they were to battle the very next morning.

"Hey there, brother. I came to help."

Eli turned around and shouted, "Charlie!"

The man with the backpack walked down from the tree line and greeted Eli with a hug. Janice walked away from the circle and joined Eli and Charlie while the remaining two members of the circle looked on confused about why this man was here and from where he had come.

"I wondered if you would come," said Eli.

"I could not here be before, Eli. You should've known that. I couldn't have shaken you awake in my way. It took Love to wake you both up, didn't it?"

As he said this he stared directly at Amy and gave her a nod and a warm smile. "Thank you." He said.

"Eli, who is this?" asked Farron.

"I'm sorry. Come over here, Charlie. This is Farron and... well, you named her. But we call her Amy.

"Pleased to meet your acquaintance, Farron and Amy." replied Charlie.

"Charlie is a dear friend of ours and this land. He lives in Pioneer Forest across the river and comes to visit... well, he comes to visit whenever he knows he might be needed. Charlie probably knows about what is going on down there at the river more so than we do, because when I say he lives in Pioneer forest, I mean he really lives in that forest, completely off the land. He hunts that side of the woods and stays by the river generally."

"So you have been living down there with Jack?" asked Amy.

"Yes, in a sense. I live apart from him and I am very quiet when I am near him. Neither of them knew I was even there until... well, I spoke to him less than an hour ago."

"You spoke to who?" asked Farron.

"Jack." Charlie responded.

There was a gasp among the crowd of friends. How could he have just spoke to Jack?   They all wondered, except Eli and Janice.

"How did he look, Charlie?" asked Eli.

"You have a job on your hands, Eli. He is nearly completely gone. The Shadow has a powerful hold on him and has no intention of letting go. He came after me and I was able to knock him to the ground enough to speak to him. He wanted to fight more. But the Shadow pulled him back. My guess is that the Shadow knows exactly what is going on up here and is training Jack hard to get ready for when you all go down there."

"What do you mean, 'you all'? You have to go with us! We can use all the help we can get." said Amy.

"I am happy to help Amy. But my assistance will have to be given from up here. I am here to tend this fire and to be a guide for all of you as you embark tomorrow."

"What? Eli, if this guy is going to help, we need him down there with us don't we?" asked Farron.

"Farron, I cannot fight this battle. I can only protect you from Jack in one way and that is by killing him. It is my understanding that you all want to save him."

"Well then, help us save him!" said Amy.

"I have a history with the Shadow. If I go there and threaten the Shadow's work in any way he will use Jack first to run me off and then I will have to kill the Shadow, after I kill Jack."

"Well, if we can save Jack, then I don't care what the hell you do to the Shadow!" said Farron.

"If I kill the Shadow, the land will go down with it. The Shadow must be run off the land. To kill it, is to change the course of the Universe in a way that you do not want to mess with. The ultimate power I have is useful. But, it is only useful in the scenario that you are all going to die and the land may be taken over by the Shadow. At that point, I can kill the Shadow. But the land goes with it."

"That's not much of an option, Charlie." said Amy.

Charlie nodded at her in simple agreement and turned his attention to Eli. This was the way it was whether they liked it or not. Charlie was finished explaining and changed the subject swiftly once he had Eli's attention.

"Are the rocks ready, Eli?"

"Yeah, Charlie they're ready. Would you care to keep the fire?"

"I thought you'd never ask."

The circle of people around the fire came back together with the new member and after a few moments of silence, Eli handed the pitchfork over to Charlie and waved the smoke of the burning sage over him and the fork itself. Charlie did the same for Eli and then Eli waved the smoke over the rest of the group. As they each began to lower their bodies to the earth, and crawl inside the little door on the lodge, Charlie began tearing the fire down in order to get the hot rocks out. He looked strong, his silhouette standing proudly in the sparks and flames against the night sky. With pitchfork in hand, he thrust it deep inside the burning coals and came out with a glowing red rock. He held the big fork horizontal to himself and leaned toward the burning stone, blowing the hot ashes and loose coals back into the inferno until the rock was clean of any debris that could smoke up the lodge or fly off and burn someone.

Once everyone was inside, the rocks whistled and sung their songs, a high-pitched whine as they do when they are red hot. The heat filled the lodge and dried the air almost immediately. Again, some time went by in complete silence and then the drum. "Boom Boom Boom" The rattle hissed and Eli spoke.

"Tonight we are brought together, brothers and sisters, for the greatest conflict that has ever plagued this place that so many people call home. Our brother, Jack is lost in the woods and we have tasked ourselves with bringing him home. This lodge will be hot and I expect that we will stay inside it all night. I plan to sleep here with the rocks inside the womb of our great Mother until morning. The lodge is an introspective experience for each person. But, it is a place for positive intentions. So, I want each and every one of your intentions to be made clear in the door to the east which is the door for new beginnings. We are not the Lakota people, which is where I understand this ceremony to have come from. So, we will not begin our door in the west as do they. We will always begin our first door in the east and work our way to the west out of respect for our ancestors as well as theirs."

The lodge then broke out into the beautiful song that Jack once, so enjoyed. They sang as loud as they could. There was no keeping pitch or keeping time as is tradition in western music. There was only a loud boisterous praise to their understanding of a creator. It was a pleasant singing to the ears of someone who understood. It truly was a "joyful noise".

****

From inside the mouth of the cave, Jack heard the singing going on at the top of the bluffs. He heard the noise and it reminded him again of that something sweet. He was sure that he had been up there before. He was sure that his lungs had belted out sounds such as that. But he was too far away from that now. It was only a distant spark in his mind that he could not keep lit. The Shadow was always there to snuff that spark out for him. It was to keep him focused, to keep him alive and to make him stronger and more powerful with each passing day. The singing continued. It only stopped for short intervals and Jack could hear banging and booming going on and muffled speech only when the people up there raised their voices loud enough for Jack to catch a syllable; And then the singing, again.

They are getting ready for you, Jack. They are getting ready to come and take you away from me.

"I hear them, Shadow. Why do they scream like that?"

They want you dead. They want to take your power that I gave you and use it themselves.

Jack lie silently and still on the hard rocky floor of the damp cavern and listened to the singing. There was something tickling his cheek. What is this? He placed his hand to his cheek and jerked it back. It was something wet and warm. *A tear... that is what it is.*

It's a tear! Jack remembered what it was. But he could not make heads or tails as to how he knew what it was. Nor, did he remember the last time he had seen one. But, he instinctively knew that if he put it to his tongue, it would taste salty.

Don't do silly things like that, Jack! That time is over! Roared the Shadow.

Jack wiped the tear on the rocky floor of the cave. He wanted to taste it. He wanted to remember that taste of a salty tear. But he dared not do such things under the Shadow's watchful eye. He just lay still, as still as could be. Movement angered the Shadow. Movement was only to be used in the event that there was some other place to be or something to kill. Speaking aloud was unfavorable in the Shadow's eyes as well. When Jack spoke aloud, he was chastised. The Shadow prefers to speak from within the mind. The Shadow wanted control of the mind and this is where Jack knew he drew his new amazing strength from. It was from the Shadow's constant speaking to him through his thoughts.

Jack wanted to crawl back into the belly of the cave where the Shadow lived and breathed. He wanted to see this magnificent creature that spoke to him constantly. He imagined what he may look like. He thought of the Shadow as sort of a god and wondered if he must look like most gods. *Is he strong and powerful, muscular and always ready to give power and protect his children from harm?* The Shadow read his thoughts.

Not yet young man. You are not yet ready to see me. You still have more work to do.

"Yes, Shadow."

Jack could not understand why he was not to lay eyes upon his new powerful deity. But, he accepted it as law, only because the Shadow had said it.

****

Back in the ancient ceremony of the Lodge, the group of friends prayed together that Jack would be saved and that they would remain safe. They made their intentions clear. They sang and they became one with one another. They became a unified force for the good of the land on which they sat. Eli and Janice were revived with purpose and intent after having been lost for so many months, wandering the land and the house with nothing to save and no mission to accomplish. Now, a new fire burned within them all. Farron had not thought about a drink in quite some time and now even if the thought would enter his mind, it would only appear as something that would hinder his progress, his purpose. A new Farron emerged from within him. It was one that he never knew existed, a powerful man with ageless experience at life, a kind heart that served mankind and a fierce protector; a warrior for a peaceful existence. He felt unstoppable and a new solidarity resided inside him. It was the simple knowledge that this is who he had become and he was making the decision to remain this person for the rest of his days. It was someone he liked to be after having spent so many years being someone that he hated. Amy had completely immersed herself in the purpose of love. Every action, every word would come from love. There was no fear. She contained none of the terrible debilitating thing. Amy was conscious, aware and present in every moment as a powerful force of pure unconditional love. Together, this how they stood the greatest chance of saving Jack and they knew it to be so.

Eli spoke up. "After the fourth and final door to the west, my new friends, we will rest in this place until the sun rises. When it does, we will leave here with one purpose, one mission, and one goal. Amy will lead us north down to the river. Farron, you will stay directly to the west of the group in case Jack attacks from the edge of the bluff. Janice and I will be in the rear of the formation. Janice, I will need you to open your mind to any presence of fear and alert us as to where it is coming from. If you sense that fear, it is Jack coming for us. Remember; do not kill Jack unless there is no other way. Farron will be the first line of defense against an attack and I will step in to help him hold Jack. Janice will keep her mind open and communicate with Charlie about what the Shadow is saying to him and Amy will have to be the negotiator. Amy, he will not negotiate at first. You know that, as well as I do. But you must keep trying. You must not give up."

Everyone soaked up Eli's words like they soaked up the heat. There was no misunderstanding what was to happen. Everyone was perfectly clear and set firm in their mind to follow through with their own tasks to make the mission of the group a swinging success. Although considerable doubt existed within the world of chance, they could not acknowledge that world or any doubt, itself. They could only acknowledge that they were as prepared as ever and intent on going forward down to the river and coming back with Jack or not coming back at all. Every mind in the small space was set on the same idea.

As the rocks began to cool, Charlie put two more in with the pitchfork and then crawled into the lodge himself after building the fire back up to last all night. He pulled the canvas door down to meet the cool dirt floor for the purpose of holding in the heat. All that could be heard inside the womb was the occasional sniff or a sigh from one of the five occupants. Not a word was spoken for the rest of the evening. Not a lot of sleep was to be had either although they all knew that they needed it. They were all just simply too anxious to sleep soundly. It was more of a time for reflection and personal preparedness. Sleep would come when the time was right. It would creep upon the body when the body did not expect it. Like a stalker in the night, it would reach in to steal their consciousness and leave them breathing deep and slumbering in their den.

****

The morning came on quickly. No one in the lodge felt that they had gotten the sleep they had hoped for. Regardless of the lack of sleep, the strong sense of purpose never waned; they were all ready to meet the day with whatever it held in store. Stretches and yawns were heard in the small enclosed space and the heat of the brittle stones still emanated vaguely throughout the lodge. The smells of sweet grass and clove still hung in the dry air and their bodies carried the sweet smell of it deep within their pores. The sweat had cleansed them and they were fresh and new to the world, ready to fight and prepared to win or die for the cause that stood taller and greater than any one of them.

Charlie reached around and flung the canvas door up, resting it on top of the lodge. On his hands and knees, he crawled out and put his lips to the ground, kissing it in an acknowledgement and an honor to his sustainer, the Earth. He stood slowly to meet the morning air and the sliver of sunlight on the eastern horizon. It peeked back at him as if to cheer him on and to beg him to pull back the blanket of clouds brought on by the Shadow so that it may reveal its bright beauty back to the landscape it loved to warm. Charlie listened closely to his Mother and followed her sweet bidding.

The other four crawled out of the lodge without a word only a moment or so after Charlie. He was building back the fire that was reduced to a small flame on a bed of coals throughout the evening. They all knelt by it, warming their hands and soaking up the morning air. Amy was the first to utter a word.

"Well, I will not ask if you are all ready. I know you are. Let's pack up everything we need and start making our way down to the river."

"I love you, Sis."

"I love you too, Farron. No matter what happens here today, I love each and every one of you. Now let's go get Jack."

JEREMY NICHOLAS

CHAPTER TWENTY-TWO

With Amy out front, the four of them broke through the tree line and started making their way down the lonely trail to the river. The leaves on the trees had yet to make it much past budding because of the lack of sunlight emitted here; the canopy of forest made it doubly hard to get sufficient light to the starved trees. The Shadow's effect on the once vibrant forest was extremely evident. Last year's dead leaves were on the ground almost as much as they still clung. Everything had been thrown out of concert and it was obvious that it would take time to recover.

Their feet crunched in the dead leaves on the ground and Farron, standing directly to the west of the group, kept his eyes peeled for any movement coming from that direction. He was certain Jack would hear them coming with the rustling of the leaves on the ground.

"Try hard and pick your feet up high as you walk." He told them.

The group did as he said and it brought their approach to a less audible level. The fight was going to happen regardless of their ability to be stealthy. Farron understood that; but the less of a drop that Jack could get on them, the better their chances at success.

As the trail ascended in altitude by only a little, the trees grew slightly less thick against the edges of the trail. The wind had blown across here and the trail was less covered in the noisy rattling leaves. Over this part, they tried hard to step on the solid dirt. Eli watched Farron closely and still kept his peripheral vision and attention focused on the other remaining degrees of space that surrounded the group. Janice kept in contact with Charlie who sat back at the fire and constantly sent the group positively reinforcing thoughts.

Janice you are strong, strong enough for this and you are a brave and fearless woman. Jack is your brother and you will stop at nothing to save him. Janice, he would do the same for you; would he not?

It was a welcome reassuring truth of which Janice was certain. Jack would do this for her. He would do this a thousand times over for her and never regret it, not for one moment.

The group trudged on and in as much silence as possible. As the trail began to descend, it split in two. One path led to Snake Cave, named that not because it is infested with snakes, but because it slithers through the Ozark Mountains for miles and miles. It is one of the longest caves in this part of the country. The other path led down to the river, which is where they headed.

Making the left turn down the lonely path, a sickness set in that each of them felt. It was a heavy sickness that rained down upon them. It was almost as dark as night in this part of the woods and they could feel the earth tremble steadily as they continued down the path. Farron's eyes were wide and his head moved as if it was on a swivel. He looked up and down the western side of their path. It was dead silent. He knew Jack was going to leap from the edge of that bluff at any moment. He wished he could know when; but he knew he would never be afforded that luxury.

In the midst of the dark and the silence, a fog began to rise. It seemed to rise from the earth itself and not to have come down from the sky as it should have. Furthermore, they were too high up from the river for the fog to rest here at the top of the bluff. Then the stench of it smacked them hard and watered their eyes. A heavy wind slammed into them from the north and it immediately left and fell back to the earth. It was as if some gigantic creature blew a huge breath of air at them. They all stopped in their tracks.

"Charlie says we are close." said Janice.

"We must be. I am assuming everyone can smell that." replied Amy.

They all nodded and agreed that the smell of sulfur was thick in the air. Everyone stood where they were and tried their best to acclimate to the new disgusting environment. Rubbing their eyes and peering through the thick fog, they agreed that Jack may be very close and this was the Shadow's way of concealing his approach.

"Use it to your advantage, Farron," said Amy

"I will, Sis. I know he is close by."

"Up ahead, we will break off to the right and go down the far side of the bluff," said Eli. "That should be our best shot at flanking him. Janice, ask Charlie what he thinks about that."

After a short moment passed by, Janice opened her eyes. "He said that it will not hurt to do that. But, they already know we are here. Jack is waiting for us."

A chill traveled down each respective spine and not an eye was caught without looking around wildly to see if Jack could be seen. There was nothing though, as far as they could see. A boulder would appear to be a person crouched. A tall stump would appear to be a person standing or a knot on a log would seem to be Jack ready to pounce from a tree. But all the shapes turned out to not be him.

Down the far side of the bluff they walked. It was a slower approach. But it was less steep and safe to everyone involved, even Jack, if he should attack them here. They kept up, not only for their own safety, but the safety of Jack as well, at all times. They were careful not to make a sound or as little sound as possible. As they descended the bluff down the river, a sharp turn to the left came up quickly. It was only fifty feet to the bottom. But, it was two hundred and fifty feet back to the top. There was no turning around and they would have to get in a single file line because of the width of the new path. With Farron no longer able to guard them at the west, they fell in line and moved forward.

Amy, still in front, peered around the corner as she took the next step and immediately was slapped hard and thrown back into the others. Farron got up quickly and stared with intent rage at the corner.

"Here he is!" he screamed

"Remember, Farron! Alive!" Amy yelled from the ground.

Farron leapt over Amy and rushed around the corner. *Nothing... Where is he?* He looked up and holding on to the rocks directly above his head was a beast that he could not believe he had spoken to only months earlier. Jack was terrifying. Almost completely nude, covered in callouses and scars, some still wet with blood, he held tight from the rocky ledge almost totally upside down and still as ever. His ugly face gleamed with white milky cataracts as large as saucers. They stared directly into Farron's soul from only six inches away. Suddenly, Jack's lower jaw dropped as if it had been snapped in two, right there. He screamed into Farron's face a scream that Farron could only liken unto the one they heard not long ago from their camp. It was a human's vocal chords making an inhuman sound, a miserable scream that could only be born of a type of terrible pain that only Jack had experienced and somehow coped with in this way, by being the servant of his Shadow.

Jack pounced upon Farron. But this time, Farron did not go down. He braced himself hard on his own right leg by extending it backward and planting it with great force against the rocky ground. As Jack fought him, though, that leg kept inching backward toward the edge. Eli sprung forward around Janice and Amy. He ran as hard as he could to get to Farron before he went over the bluff. As soon as he reached him, Eli jumped and simultaneously threw his arm around Jack, both of them crashing to the trail below. Farron lost his footing and fell backward landing halfway over the edge. The big man's breath was knocked out of him.

Janice spoke softly to Charlie and Amy screamed to Jack. "Remember us Jack! Remember the people that love you! You don't want this, Jack! There is a way out!"

Jack could not hear her. He was consumed with killing Eli, destroying them all one by one. He pinned Eli's arms back hard against the ground and raised his head backward.

"Can't you see I love you, brother?" screamed Eli. Jack stopped, still holding him down and lowered his head to Eli's until the tip of their noses touched. Saliva fell from Jack's loose quivering lips. He spoke in a growling roar that was nothing like his own voice.

"I... am not... your... brother!" Jack raised his head back up once again and Eli exposed his throat, not thinking. Just as the thought crossed his mind that he was exposing his throat, Jack came down hard and sunk his teeth deep into Eli's neck.

Farron, back up and breathing, fell crashing down on both of them. All three rolled down the path, Jack still attached to Eli by the teeth. Blood poured slowly now from around Jack's mouth. Eli could make no sound but a scream; Farron could not get them detached.

Amy screamed from the trail, "Jack! No! Stop it Jack!"

Charlie spoke to Janice, *Go, take the chance and go.*

Janice sprung up from her position and ran as hard as she could, holding back nothing and expelling every ounce of oxygen in her body. As she approached the three men piled up with Jack on top, she reared her right foot back as far as possible, swung it forward and made a shattering contact with the side of Jack's skull. Jack and Eli immediately separated and Jack flew through the air headfirst spitting blood and flesh. Eli lay still, eyes wide and spouting blood from the open wound on his neck. Jack lay motionless at the bottom of the trail, near the stream of the Shadow's flowing saliva that ran to the river. It gushed, again, from the mouth of the cave. The stench was strong and the wind screamed through the river valley.

Farron jumped up and ran toward Jack, heaving every breath he could muster. Upon reaching him he fell to his knees and lay across him, hoping to pin him to the ground. Jack was unconscious. But, Farron knew it wouldn't be for long. Janice rushed to Eli, helping him up. He wore a look of shock upon his face. He placed his hand over the wound and drew back a hand covered in warm blood. It would require attention quickly. But there was no time.

"C'mon!" he yelled to Janice and Amy.

They followed Eli down to Jack and Farron and just as Jack began to wake and struggle, Eli grasped his right arm. Farron let up and grasped his left and they pinned Jack down to the Earth. Janice held to the wound on Eli's neck to slow the blood as much as possible and ground her foot into Jack's right knee to keep it extended so that he couldn't kick. Amy straddled his left knee. Jack was now fully awake, blind to the pain on the right side of his head and filled with rage, ready to kill. But he could not move.

Get up! The Shadow screamed. Get up you worthless kid! What are you doing to me, Jack! Jack, you are going to fail me! Get up!

Jack tried with all his might to move the people off of him. He spat and growled. He tried to reach their veins with his teeth and tear their flesh. But they were just out of reach. Farron looked down and saw Jack snapping his teeth. He brought them down with such force that Farron knew he was going to shatter them. Quickly, he used one hand to grab a nearby stick and waited for Jack to open his mouth once more to try and take another bite. As soon as he did, Farron rammed the stick horizontally as far back into his jaws as possible. The stick hooked Jack's back molars and stayed put, allowing him to breathe but not bite down. Jack screamed back at him a terrible scream that they had all heard.

It wasn't long before Jack couldn't scream because of the stick. Nor could he bite. All he could do was breathe. Swallowing, although possible, was quite a task as well. His eyes jumped about wildly and began to make contact with Farron. They were still milky white, only the slightest remembrance of his iris was visible. Farron spoke to him directly acknowledging him as Jack. Jack flung his head the other way.

Amy sat and waited patiently until he looked at her. When his face met hers, she reached into the pack she carried and pulled out a notebook. She opened it to what seemed to be somewhere in the middle and began to read.

"I thought... 'And this is what it comes to, an abrupt end in the cycle of life. You wake up and your whole life is behind you.' She built her every dream and loving thought around that man and he was gone in an instant."

A deep bellowing wretched scream burst from within the cave. The Shadow had spoken clearly. But, Amy was speaking clearly as well. She did all she could to speak to Jack's heart, however much of it may be left. He stopped his writhing immediately and glared directly in her eyes. She could not tell if he appreciated what he had heard or if he was only thinking of another way to kill her. But she knew beyond doubt that she had gotten his full attention. The words were familiar, as they should have been. They were taken directly from his journal. Amy had snatched it from Eli's tree house days ago.

"I'm sorry I left you in the snow, Jack. I did not know it would affect you so much. I thought of you as a sweet boy, Jack. But, we were friends, confused little kids. I did not mean to break your heart!"

Jack's eyes filled with tears and as they did, the white milky films fell out of the sockets. Janice wiped them from his cheek and when his eyes opened, they were as green as the early June summer should have been. He blinked over and over, still not uttering a sound. Jack gasped for air and filled his lungs full for the first time in months.

Jack, what have you done? Look what I have given you, Jack and you just throw it away? Jack, my boy, come back to me, son! Why are doing this to me? Jack, why? The Shadow wept.

Farron reached down carefully and tested Jack by placing a finger in his mouth. Jack did not try to bite. He did not growl back. His tears just splashed to the ground and he heaved for air. Farron removed the stick.

"Shut-up! Shut-up! Shut-up!" Jack screamed back, out loud.

He is talking to the Shadow, Janice. Let him do it. Let him banish the Shadow from his mind. It has to be Jack to give the permission.

Janice let the others know what Charlie had said and they continued to hold him down until Janice said it was okay. They let him argue with the Shadow for as long as he needed. He screamed back at the Shadow over and over. He screamed obscenity after obscenity, calling the Shadow out on everything it had done to him, everything it had taken away, every part of him it had destroyed. He arched his back in pure frustration and screamed at the top of his lungs. But this time, not only was it a semi-human voice, it soon melted into only human. There was nothing horrible about this scream. It was pure desperation and full release.

Jack's arched body fell hard back to the earth and he sobbed uncontrollably.

Janice, let him go. The Shadow is separated from him now. But, watch him very closely and stay with me.

A smile made its way across her pretty face and she said, "We did it, I think. Let him go."

The other three let go of Jack and stood up around him. Eli extended a hand downward and said, "Stand up, brother." Jack took his hand and as Eli lifted him to his feet, he winced in pain and looked scared and confused. Eli put his arm around Jack and held him up. Janice did the same from the other side. Jack accepted the help.

"What happened, Eli?"

"Jack, you have been gone for some time now."

"I want to go home, Eli."

"That is precisely where you are going." said Janice

Chapter Twenty-Three

From atop the bluff they walked south back up the leafy trail. The ground still quaked from the Shadow's anger from deep with in the bowels of the rumbling cave. It was still there. It would stay there for some time until it starved from not having a host from which to feed. They would be careful for quite a while not to go back inside that cave. But, once the creature left, it would be back to its normal whispering and slithering about the ground until it could find its next human to feed on.

For now, the sun shone through the trees for the first time in a long while. Jack broke away slowly from Eli and Janice's grasp and turned back to the north looking back at the edge of the bluff. Eli and Janice stood frozen with dismay. He began walking toward the bluff, when Janice spoke up.

"Jack, No!"

Janice, let him go to the edge. I think he is still simply confused. Remember the decision is his. Said Charlie.

Jack continued his walk. The remaining four friends looked at him, hoping he would make the decision to come back. As he stopped a few feet from the edge, the bright afternoon sun spread its amber glow over the trees and across the forest floor. The woods were illuminated by the bright beautiful sun that they had not witnessed in what seemed like an eternity of darkness. A dark spot was cast behind Jack. The sun was at his face and it cast his shadow behind him.

"Do you want to go back?" Amy had walked up behind him against the advice of Charlie and Janice. But Love has no limits and she could not just let him walk away without a reason.

Jack remained peering over the bluff. He stood as still as a statue, not moving an inch for several seconds. He breathed a deep breath outward and followed it with his tears. Without turning around, he said, "No. I want to understand why I went in the first place."

"Fear, Jack. The answer to why any of us go there is always Fear. Everything you have been angry about in your life can be traced back to it. We are afraid that there may not be enough of whatever we want. But, there is always enough. We are afraid that we aren't enough, ourselves. But Jack, we are always enough. We are always worthwhile and to know that is good as long as we always keep room to grow."

"What now?" Jack asked.

"First of all, we need to get you back home and clean you up, get you fed, things like that."

"No Amy. I don't think you understand. I killed Hero. I murdered my Hero. What now? What is there left for me to do?"

He hung his head in shame. He had bared his soul to her. He had told her the one secret that would probably hurl him back into the cave once again. *They'll have nothing to do with me if they know I killed Hero. What use am I now?* But, if he hadn't told her the truth, he knew fully well that the guilt would put him back in the cave just the same. It may have happened a little slower though, giving him at least a breath of what he remembered now to be so wonderful.

"I know what you did Jack. You will have to pay for that action as well."

"How, Amy? How do I pay for that?"

"Jack, we should really discuss this later."

He turned around toward her and put her hand on his heart. He then placed his hands on her shoulders and looked into her eyes. Her eyes darted away until she heard him say her name.

"Amy." She looked back at him. His face was twisted with concern and fear. The last thing he needed was to be afraid and Amy knew that. She felt she had no other choice but to tell him the truth about his plight; about what he must do to make peace with himself and with the Universe.

"Jack, the only way you make it right, is to create again what you destroyed; except it must be better than it was before. How do you think I became love? Jack, you are now Hero and we have a lot of work to do."

****

There was, in fact, a lot of work to do. It would take a full month for Jack to recover. While his muscles had become extremely fit and strong, it was a strength to which the rest of his body had not yet grown accustomed. His mind was scarred deeply from his time in the belly of the cave with his Shadow and the fact that he had killed Hero. This was the most difficult part for Jack. He barely remembered anything that led up to it. But, he distinctly remembered firing the pistol and Hero looking back at him, hurt and confused. He could vividly see Hero's chest open from the bullet tearing through.

At the time, the Shadow screamed so deeply inside him that there seemed no way to stop himself. The Shadow was his life giving blood and he was terrified to let go of it for fear that he may wither and die out there all alone. The ranch and his friends were only a mile up the road. But, they might as well have been a million miles away. Going in, Jack only knew of Eli and Janice being present at the ranch and they seemed as lost as he was.

Amy stayed by his side as well as Farron, Eli and Janice. They all worked together to get Jack back to himself until it came time for Jack to become the Hero. When that time came, Eli took Jack to the Lodge and helped him find his mission. It was a hot lodge and inside, Jack did transform. The door flung back to the morning sun and Jack stepped out, renewed and fresh. He had a purpose and let all the guilt he carried burn up in the fire that heated the stones.

The celebration afterward was wonderful. It was as if Jack had never been in the cave at all and was still left with all of the knowledge and power of having gone through the entire ordeal. It did not change overnight, however. It took a lot of work. It took a ton of dedication and during that time, Jack and Eli worked together daily. Amy stayed away from him at times and Jack didn't like her being gone. But, she distracted him and it was best that he focus.

He thought the world of this girl who had picked him up on the side of the road and then came to his rescue at the lowest point in his life. He had asked her time and time again, "Amy, did you know you would save me when we first met? Or, was this all by chance?"

"Let's leave that to guess, Jack. Some things are more enjoyable to wonder about than they are to understand."

Jack hated this response. But, he knew that was what he was going to get, regardless. Amy didn't really like to explain things. She liked things to explain themselves. She was good for him and he knew it. When she knew he needed to work with Eli, she stepped away no matter what excuses he came up with to keep her around. She seemed to have a goal for him and Jack prayed silently to himself that her goal for him included her. He was in love in a way that he had never been before. His heart ached at the thought of her as it did when they were only children and he watched her drive away. He wondered if that was a premonition to what his life would be like with Amy. *Am I always going to be torn in two by her leaving? Will she ever stay and how the hell do I ask her to stay?*

CHAPTER TWENTY-FOUR

Night fell upon the ranch two months after the battle at the cave for Jack's life. September brought cooler night temperatures with it. Only a few nights had Jack stoked the fire in the bunkhouse. Those few times, it was more for something to do and because he missed the blazing fires that he would soon sit by in the winter, wherever he may be, as it set in.

Jack sat up tonight wondering about that very thing. *Where will I go from here?* The answer was far from him. He felt like he owed his life to Eli and Janice and the ranch. But, he knew them well enough to know that they would want him to move forward and find a path to spread light over a world in so much darkness. There were millions of other people battling daily with their own Shadows and Amy had made it clear that Jack was to become a Hero which Jack understood to mean that he must help others. He must help make the world a better place to atone for what he had done. Jack just wasn't sure if he was to do that here or if he was supposed to do it somewhere else. The thought of it made him tired. He had processed so much lately that his mind felt like it had been overrun with details and emotions that he had not considered in years, and some of them he had never considered.

Jack sat tired in his chair. But he was proud. He was alive and ready to go to war for the betterment of the entire world. He was a warrior for all that is great and good in the Universe. He just did not know where to start.

Jack laid his coffee cup down on the table beside his chair and opened the flu on the little stove to let the heat escape so as to not wake up in the middle of the night, too hot to go back to sleep. He could still hear the crackle of the fire, though and it sounded peaceful to him. The only thing better would be for a light rain to come pouring in and spatter the tin roof above. Its spattering would certainly push him over the edge of sleepiness into sweet unconsciousness.

Everything he needed save the bathroom and shower was contained in this little room. As he left his chair, Jack blew out the oil lamp that sat on the table and stepped quietly across the room, crawling in between his cold sheets. He loved to be between two cool sheets and safe in his bed. This place was as far from the cruel uncomfortable cave as he could get. Jack closed his eyes and emptied his mind of everything except the river. He imagined himself standing by it in the night. He could almost hear it rushing by and splattering itself upon the rocky banks. He imagined the moon striking the water with its magnificent blue light and sending a long line of it down river as far as he could see. He listened to the chirping crickets in his mind and waited for a small mouth bass to break the surface of the black water. His breathing grew deeper and slower. His mind began to drift. Then, Jack heard the door to the bunkhouse creak open.

"Jack," he heard her whisper.

"W...w...who's there?" he stuttered. But he knew it was Amy. Jack was just at a loss for words.

His heart pounded for her to be coming to see him. *Why is she here? Does she want to talk? Did I make her mad and is she coming to tell me all about it? What is she here for?*

Amy tip-toed in the room and whispered, "Jack it's me, Amy."

"I know." he whispered back.

Silence abounded for a moment until Amy returned a whisper. "Then why did you ask who it was?"

"Why are we still whispering?" he replied

"I don't know." she said still in a whisper.

Jack paused with a lack of knowing what to say next and they both chuckled over the awkward moment. Jack sat up in his bed and watched her come around the corner by the light of a single candle that burned on his nightstand. She was gorgeous to him. Every time he was in her presence, he thought himself useless in so many ways. But he was sure that she made him better. He was positive that she was good for him. But, he knew that the decision couldn't be made by him to know whether this was a good thing or not. He could not see it objectively. He was blinded by his love for her.

"Amy, what's going on?"

"I wanted to come see you, Jack. Is that alright?"

"Of course it is!" he almost yelled.

"Shhh! You're going to wake everyone up."

"Sorry, Amy."

He was afraid to follow his heart. But he felt like it was now or never. He had to tell her how he felt before she walked away from him again.

"Amy, sit down."

"Is that an order Jack, or a request; because I do not take orders very well."

"Shit. Amy, I didn't mean it that way. Will you please sit down?"

"Jack, don't take me so seriously. I am just giving you a hard time."

Amy sat down on the bed with Jack and he reached forward and placed his hand on her shoulder.

"Amy, I want you to understand how I feel about you and if you do not want to hear it, feel free to leave at any time. I am not holding you here."

"Okay?"

"I have lost you twice in my life and I have no intention of ever going through that again. I do not know where you want to go on your path because you have not made that clear to me. But Amy, if I am going to be a Hero to anyone, I would really like to start with you."

"Well Jack, that's going to be a big job." Amy replied jokingly."

Jack didn't know what to think. He didn't know if she was ignoring his advance or if she was oblivious to it.

"Amy, I love you. I want you and I want you to be with me."

"You mean you want have sex?" Amy said loudly in an attempt to embarrass him a little more.

"No!" he replied and then immediately thought better of it. "Well, yes! Of course!" He paused, realizing what he had just said and how stupid it must have sounded. "That is not what I was saying Amy. I mean, I really…"

Amy interrupted him with a response; "Jack you're too easy to mess with. I love you too."

She leaned in toward him and kissed his mouth. Jack was overcome and his heart was pounding hard. His breathing was ragged and wild and he placed his other hand on her shoulder and spun her around on the bed, crawling on top of her. She reached down to the bottom of his shirt and pulled it over his head while he pushed hers over her breasts. They held on to one another, bodies pressing hard against each other. Either of them could have stayed like this all night. They could feel the other's heart beating against their skin and neither of them had any thought of stopping. Jack and Amy tore at one another until they lay naked on top of the bed by the candlelight. When he entered her, she shuttered and he felt her warm breath against his chest. Jack had not made love in what seemed like forever and he wasted not one bit of energy in this moment. She was everything he ever wanted and he told her so as he made love with her. She believed him and lay aside all of the walls she had built to protect herself. She loved him back and when they were completely spent, they lay side-by-side, hand in hand, in silence.

The rain did eventually move in and made its sound on the roof. Except, now, Jack was not sleepy; nor was Amy. They talked the night away not worrying a bit about the coming morning or any questions they may have to answer. They held to one another like their lives depended on it and Jack's heart felt renewed, no longer lonely. It was full of love.

"So where do we go from here, Amy?"

"We go to The Bluff."

"The town?" he asked.

"Yes, Jack. We drive to The Bluff tomorrow."

"Alright, mind if I may ask why?"

"Jack, I have found something for you to do. But, more importantly, I have found an opportunity for you to make good on your purpose of becoming Hero."

"Really, Amy? What might that be?"

"Jack, as strange as it may seem, I found you, well... us a place not far from here. There is some work that just might be perfect for you. You need a way to take care of us and atone for Hero's death. It's perfect, I think. It gives you the opportunity to chase the Shadow in some of the most exciting ways you could imagine, and win."

"Seriously, I want to know what I'm supposed to do from here. You have to be serious about some things, you know." Jack still believed her to be joking with him.

"Jack, I am serious. You are going to have the opportunity to deal with people on a daily basis, people that have made some poor decisions in their lives and are like you were. You will have the chance to really help people, to be their Hero, Jack. That is the only way to get past what you have done. They are completely consumed by their Shadows. It will be your Mission to discover the caves of their own despair, in which they hide. You will chase them down and help them at a time when they are more driven by Fear, than in any other time in their lives. This will be your grandest opportunity to help them. They will be just as much or more consumed than you were. It will be your opportunity then, to battle the Shadow, showing them their power and helping them find a better way to their True selves. Inevitably, it will be up to them to break free from their Shadow and many of them will not. But, Jack, that is where you will start."

"Amy, I don't know what I think of all of that."

"Good, think about it tomorrow while I am driving you to The Bluff."

JEREMY NICHOLAS

Jeremy Nicholas was born in Homestead Florida in September of 1980. He grew up loving the outdoors and arts of all kinds, including musical instruments, writing and singing. The son of two private school teachers and the grandson of a Christian Minister, Jeremy lovingly regards himself as "The Black Sheep" of his family. And, he maintains a wonderful loving relationship with them, at the same time.

A lifetime loner of sorts, Jeremy enjoys reading, riding his Harley Davidson and writing. He is an avid outdoorsman and loves to fish at every opportunity. "I've never fished for fish, really. I fish to fish. Just like, I don't ride my Harley to get somewhere. I ride it to ride. This is the first book I've ever finished because I don't write to finish a book. I write because my life depends on it..."

Jeremy and his wife operate a Bail Bond and Legal Services Company. Although he despises the term, "Bounty Hunter", for the sake of easy explaining, that is precisely what he does. His travels all over the Nation to bring wanted fugitives back to justice, and these experiences have spawned much of his latest writing. He also volunteers his time and resources to help the needy in his community. Jeremy is a devoted family man, and loves his wife, Jessica and their two boys, Christian and Dillion, with all of his heart. They reside in a small town in the Missouri Ozarks.

www.ingramcontent.com/pod-product-compliance
Lightning Source LLC
Chambersburg PA
CBHW070105280626
47159CB00016B/1323